POPPY PYM

and the SMUGGLER'S SECRET

Also by Laura Wood:

Poppy Pym and the Pharaoh's Curse

Poppy Pym and the Double Jinx

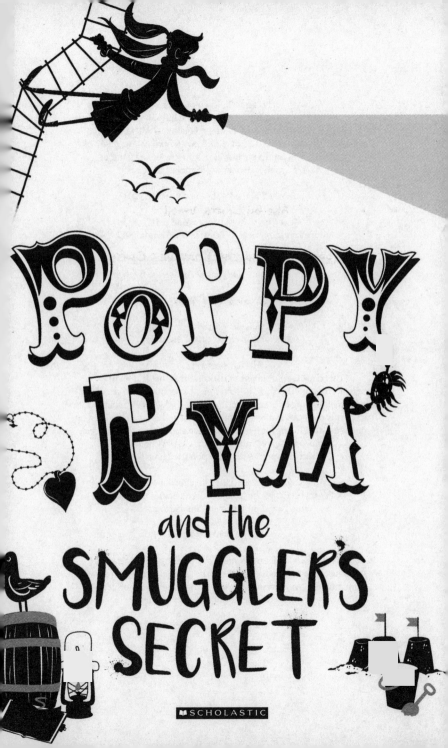

POPPY PYM

and the SMUGGLER'S SECRET

SCHOLASTIC

Scholastic Children's Books
An imprint of Scholastic Ltd
Euston House, 24 Eversholt Street, London, NW1 1DB, UK
Registered office: Westfield Road, Southam, Warwickshire, CV47 0RA
SCHOLASTIC and associated logos are trademarks and/or
registered trademarks of Scholastic Inc.

First published in the UK by Scholastic Ltd, 2017

Text copyright © Laura Wood, 2017
Illustration copyright © Beatrice Bencivenni, 2017

The right of Laura Wood and Beatrice Bencivenni to be identified as the author
and illustrator of this work has been asserted by them.

ISBN 978 1407 18018 2

A CIP catalogue record for this book
is available from the British Library.

Printed by CPI Group (UK) Ltd, Croydon, CR0 4YY
Papers used by Scholastic Children's Books are made
from wood grown in sustainable forests.

1 3 5 7 9 10 8 6 4 2

www.scholastic.co.uk

This book is dedicated to my Nan and Paps who gave me so many adventures by the sea. (And almost as many Cornish pasties.)

CHAPTER ONE

My hands were clammy, and I could hear my heart thump-thump-thumping away like the persistent beat of a catchy dance number. I glanced up and down the corridor for the hundredth time, making sure that no one was going to catch me. All was quiet and, taking a deep breath, I turned my attention to the lock on Miss Susan's door.

How had it come about that I, Poppy Pym, found myself breaking into my chemistry teacher's room? I hear you wonder. Well, that is an excellent question and you obviously have a keen detective mind yourself, to be wondering such a wonder. There is, of course, a perfectly logical explanation. In fact, I *had* actually broken into Miss Susan's room once before, when I had accused her of being a dastardly jewel thief and it turned out she was completely innocent. (As every detective knows, a red herring or two is sure to send you in the wrong direction before you capture a criminal mastermind, but I'll admit my run-in with Miss Susan was not my finest moment.) However, this time the break-in was a very different beast. For one thing, I didn't have the help of my best pals Kip Kapur and Ingrid Blammel (this particular mission was definitely something that I needed to do alone), and for another thing I wasn't trying to prove Miss Susan was a desperate criminal. No, this time I was trying to prove something much more serious ... that she was my mother.

Yes, it was all a bit loopy and if I thought about it too hard then my brain began to twirl like lots of spinning plates precariously balanced on spindly sticks.

You see, when I was a baby I was left at a travelling circus with a note from a mysterious person called "E". Then I was adopted by a fantastic and funny circus family led by ringleader, trapeze artist and psychic Madame Petronella Pym. My life *was totally normal* until I was eleven when

I was sent to Saint Smithen's boarding school. That's when things got pretty strange, and not just because I had to eat cornflakes for breakfast instead of candy floss, and learn to juggle numbers in maths class rather than flaming tennis balls with BoBo the clown. That was when I started to wonder about who had left me behind at the circus all those years ago, and Pym had given me an envelope of "clues" that had been left with me as a baby – clues which I was sure would point me towards my real mother. One of these clues was a necklace, a very distinctive necklace – a silver chain threaded with tiny pearls and a fancy engraved silver heart charm.

The thing was, I had seen this unusual necklace once before – around the neck of my chemistry teacher, and occasional nemesis, Miss Susan.

See? Pretty complicated stuff. I mean, it could be a coincidence, and she just happens to have the same antique necklace as my mother gave me. But as I know from all my reading of detective novels, coincidences that big are pretty rare.

It had been months since Pym had given me the necklace and I still hadn't told a single soul about Miss Susan. It was just too big and everything was so uncertain, I didn't even know how to start telling anyone. Saying the words out loud might make everything real, and I wasn't sure if I *wanted* any of this to be real. Did I really want Miss Susan to be my mum?

I wasn't sure *how* I felt, but I knew that I needed to start investigating. My favourite books are the Dougie Valentine detective novels by H.T. Maddox and they're all about this kid detective Dougie and his dog, Snoops. Since starting at Saint Smithen's I had become a pretty excellent detective myself – you can check out my previous cases if you want – and so I had put my top-class detective brain to work on the problem, trying to find out more about Miss Susan and her necklace. Unfortunately, almost immediately after I had been given the necklace, Miss Susan disappeared for a whole term to lecture at a fancy university in Switzerland and, let me tell you, it is definitely much harder to undertake covert surveillance on someone if they decide to leave the country and you're a twelve-year-old girl who lives in a boarding school.

While Miss Susan was away I pored over all the clues I had to work with – the necklace and the other two items that had been left with baby me. The first was a receipt for a pair of shoes (pink trainers, size six) from "Sal's Shoe Shop" in a place called Snardwell (so far I had been unable to find Snardwell on any map, despite many hours in Saint Smithen's library), and the second thing was an envelope containing a small piece of card. In the same curling handwriting that had written the note pinned to my baby blanket were the words "For Emergencies" and underneath that a long line of numbers: 09325691502763902751. I had looked at the message so many times now that I knew the long chain of numbers off by heart. But what could it mean? It was obviously some sort of code, and I had spent months trying to break it without success. By the time Miss Susan arrived back at school it was a relief to get stuck into some real, stealthy snooping and I began keeping notes of my observations of her movements. I kept my coded notes in a small, red notebook. Unfortunately so far they mostly consisted of things like:

Tuesday 1st March
  Subject ate grapefruit for breakfast. (Yuck.)

Or:

Thursday 14th April

Break time: subject had whispered conversation with Mr Grant. Attempt at closer surveillance failed due to KK's noisy accusations that people were "hogging all the biscuits". By the time I had silenced KK by stuffing chocolate digestives in his mouth, subject's conversation was over.

One useful thing that I *had* observed, though, was that Miss Susan ate her dinner at 6.30 p.m. precisely and that she remained in the dining hall until 7.15 p.m. Every single day. And so I had formulated a plan, one that could get me into a LOT of trouble, but one that might be worth the risk. It was time to do some first-rate investigating. And that brings us back to me breaking into Miss Susan's room. (See. . . I told you there was a perfectly logical explanation!) With a satisfying *click* my lock-picking wigglings succeeded and I pushed the door open. It looked like any other bedroom – although admittedly a freakishly neat and tidy one – but I knew better. This room may well be the key to unlocking the mystery of my past and I wasn't about to waste such an opportunity. My hands were shaking as I pressed the buttons on my wristwatch. There was no time to lose.

I looked at my watch: 6.36. By my calculations, Miss Susan would be sitting down with her tray of food right now. Taking a deep breath, I crossed the threshold of her room and closed the door behind me: I was in.

Miss Susan's room was predictably spotless, her bed was smooth and the sheets were tucked around the mattress in very precise corners. There wasn't much else to see, just a wardrobe, a chest of drawers and a little dressing table, and a small bookcase with a cosy armchair next to it.

I tiptoed around to the drawers beside the bed and my heart was skittering all over the place like a tambourine falling down the stairs. I knew that what I was doing was technically wrong and for a moment I hesitated, with my hand on the handle to the top drawer. *Just do it!* a voice cried inside my head. *You need some answers and they might be in this very room!* I felt the thrill of chasing a clue zap through me and I yanked the drawer open in one quick movement before I had time to talk myself out of it. There wasn't much in there – just a pen, a blank notepad, and some fancy hand cream. Silently and speedily

I checked the other drawers, the dressing table and the wardrobe. Nothing suspicious in any of them. I looked at my watch again: 6.56 p.m. I was running out of time. With a frustrated sigh I sank into the armchair and stared despondently at the bookcase.

There were a lot of boring-looking books on chemistry, and something called *Dancing on Air: the True Art of Ballroom Dancing*, and ... hang on... A shock ran through me as I spotted a group of familiar spines on the bottom shelf. Who knew Miss Susan was a Dougie Valentine fan? Maybe we did have something in common after all. I spotted all of my favourites: *Dougie Valentine and the Lost Sock of Terror*, *Dougie Valentine and the Ham Sandwich of Doom*, *Dougie Valentine and the Alligator of Destiny*. Miss Susan even had the very first Dougie Valentine book, *Dougie Valentine and the Handkerchief of Horror*, and it looked almost as battered as my own copy. Pulling the book from the shelf I flicked through the well-thumbed pages – and watched, frozen, as something fluttered to the floor.

It was a photograph – an old-looking photograph. With a trembling hand I picked it up, and turned it over. The world wobbled around me, and all the air

8

felt like it had been sucked out of the room as I read the words that were written there.

CHAPTER TWO

In my hand was a slightly faded polaroid photograph and looking out at me from this photograph was Miss Susan. She looked like she was in her early twenties and her expression was quite serious as she stared into the camera. Around her neck was the now familiar necklace with the heart charm, and in her arms was . . . a baby.

A small, squishy, red-faced baby wrapped in a soft yellow blanket. The baby's arm was reaching up towards Miss Susan's face, its little pudgy hand waving in the air. On the back of the picture in smudged green ink were the words "Me and my daughter".

So it was true. Miss Susan was my mother.

Me and my daughter

I was gaping silently at the picture, my mind as empty as a cracked bucket when a shrill beeping noise filled the room. In a daze I realized that the sound was coming from my wrist, or more accurately from the alarm on my watch, which I had set to go off at 7.10 p.m. I jumped clumsily to my feet, discovering that my knees were having a good old wobble, and shoved the Dougie Valentine book back on to the shelf with fumbling fingers, tucking the photograph into my pocket. I ran to the door and pressed my ear against it, listening hard for any sound in the corridor outside. All was silent and I opened the door a crack, listening again before slipping out and pulling it shut behind me, the lock clicking back into place. With a sigh I slumped against the door. I had done it.

"No running in the hallways, Callum!" A familiar, chilly voice reached my ears and I snapped to attention. Darting around the corner, in the opposite direction to the voice, I tried to be as silent as possible. As the sound of footsteps got nearer I held my breath to prevent even the teensiest hint of a sound escaping me, and when I could feel my face going purple I tried to take short, quiet little breaths instead. Unfortunately, to my ears I sounded like a wheezing accordion and I fully expected to feel an angry hand on my shoulder at any moment. Inching towards the end of the wall I peeked back around the corner. There she was. Miss Susan.

My mother.

Because, as my jittery brain was shouting at me very loudly and not very calmly, that is who she must be, and the proof was burning a hole in my pocket. (Metaphorically of course, I don't mean I had accidentally set the photograph on fire because then I really would have been failing to remain inconspicuous, what with standing in a hallway while flames burst from my shorts.)

I peeped at Miss Susan, trying – as I had for the last few months – to see any similarities between us. Miss Susan is quite short and she has blonde hair. I am tall for my age and have hair that is more of a light mousy-brown colour. Miss Susan is very neat and dainty. She usually wears white clothes that anyone else would spill chocolate ice cream down immediately, but which always look like she has just come back from the dry cleaners. I looked down at my own outfit. I had changed out of my school uniform and into my own clothes before dinner and the effect was far from pristine. A favourite cosy green jumper with holes in the elbows, and a pair of blue shorts over pink-and-black stripy tights finished off with battered trainers, one with yellow shoelaces and one with orange. The orange shoelaces were untied.

But, I told myself, there *are* the eyes. Miss Susan's eyes are pale green, just like mine. Also we both have a scattering of freckles across our noses. These were two things I must have inherited from her.

It felt strange seeing Miss Susan standing just a few metres away after my latest discovery. I had suspected that Miss Susan was my mother since I had made the connection between the necklaces, but having real proof was a whole other thing. I thought I would feel happy or excited or angry or *something*, but I just felt sort of empty like a hollowed-out pumpkin.

As I scuttled through the winding corridors back towards my room the empty feeling started to be replaced by a very full feeling, a feeling of uncertainty as my mind positively erupted with questions. If Miss Susan was my mother, why hadn't she ever told me? Why had she left me at the circus? Was it just a coincidence that I had ended up at the same school where my mother was a teacher?

I arrived at a door with a gleaming sign that read GOLDFINCHES 3 on it, and pushed it open. It seemed that I would need to squish these questions down for the time being because I was not alone – both of my roommates were there.

Ingrid was occupying her usual position, sitting on her bed, her nose stuck firmly in a large book. It was more unusual to find Letty in our room – she was usually off at one of her clubs because she seemed to be in charge of every activity that took place in the school. Letty had her back to me but she was dressed all in white with some sort of strange headgear over her dark curls. When she heard me come in she swung around, almost stabbing me in the chest with a long thin sword.

"Oof. Sorry, Poppy!" Letty's muffled voice came from behind the mask she was wearing. "Just off to fencing club!" She waved the sword around a bit.

"I didn't know we had a fencing club," I managed, dodging to the side to avoid Letty's enthusiastic sword wielding.

"Well, it's a small one – people keep leaving although I don't know why," Letty said cheerfully, knocking over a stack of books with her sword.

"Riiiight," I said. "Well, have fun!" With another sweep of her sword Letty charged out of the room in search of a duel.

At that moment Ingrid emerged, all big blinking eyes and dazed expression, from behind her book. "Poppy!" she exclaimed. "When did you get here?"

"Only just." I grinned. "In time to see some of Letty's sword-fighting skills."

"Oh." Ingrid blinked again. "Was Letty here too?"

I shook my head. Once Ingrid's brain was in a

book she was totally lost to the rest of the world and there was nothing you could do about it. She seemed to be waking up from her reading daze now, though, and had jumped to her feet, her cheeks pink and her eyes blazing with excitement. "Where have you been?" she asked, but luckily didn't give me time to answer. (Because, really, what could I have said? *"Oh, sorry, Ingrid, but I was just breaking into our chemistry teacher's bedroom where I found evidence that she's my long-lost mother who abandoned me as a baby. Nice weather we've been having, isn't it?"*)

"I've been dying to tell you!" Ingrid continued breathlessly. "Have you heard?"

"Heard what?" I asked, puzzled.

"It's all over the school." Ingrid practically hopped on the spot. "We're going on a school trip ... for a whole week ... and we're going ... to the seaside!"

CHAPTER THREE

"The seaside?!" I exclaimed. "Really?" A tiny seed of excitement appeared in my very confused and swirling mind.

Ingrid nodded. "Yes, and it's all Miss Susan's doing. Miss Susan of all people, can you believe it?"

"Miss Susan? What's she got to do with it?" I managed, my voice only sounding slightly squeaky.

Ingrid didn't seem to notice. "Some friend of hers has just inherited a CASTLE by the sea! A real castle. Stuffed full of history." Ingrid's eyes were shining but I didn't get a chance to respond before she continued. "Apparently they're opening a campsite and they needed people to come and do a trial-run holiday and Miss Susan volunteered us!"

"What . . . me and you?" I asked blankly.

"No, dummy!" Ingrid laughed. "The first years. We're going for a whole week and there's going to be rock climbing and surfing and abseiling, which sounds awful, but it doesn't matter . . . because there will also be a real life historical marvel. It's called Crumley Castle – doesn't it sound brilliant?"

I thought all the activities sounded pretty great, but I knew Ingrid wasn't the biggest fan of things that required good coordination – she always says she has two left feet. The hamster wheel of my mind was moving at warp speed and I could feel the familiar tingling of a plan coming together.

"Are you all right, Poppy?" Ingrid asked, peering closely at my face. "You've gone a strange, blotchy pink colour."

"I'm fine," I said quickly, then I tried to adopt a totally casual pose by sort of slumping my shoulders and crossing my arms. "So . . . is Miss Susan coming with us, then?" I made my voice as offhand as possible.

"Yes, Miss Susan and Mr Grant. . ." Ingrid still looked concerned. "Are you sure you're OK though? Why are you all hunched over like that? Are you feeling sick?"

Clearly my very laid-back, carefree body language wasn't doing the trick so I gave up. "Don't worry," I said with a smile. "I'm feeling better now."

And it was true; this was an unexpected development but actually it couldn't be better. A whole week away with Miss Susan, plenty of time to do some more snooping. Maybe this was also my chance to get to know Miss Susan a bit better, to find more in common with her, and, if things went really well, to ask her some of the questions that were falling all over each other in my brain. I felt my spirits rising like a helium-filled balloon.

I realized then that I had nearly fallen into a well-known detective trap – I was taking this too personally, and anyone who's ever read a detective story knows that letting emotions interfere with a case always ends in disaster. I needed to treat the situation like the mystery it was, not worry about how it made me *feel*. I would work out all the answers like a top detective and everything would turn out brilliantly. Ignoring the tiny flutter in the pit of my stomach I plastered on a big grin and began pumping Ingrid for more information about this trip.

Before it was time for lights out I slipped out of the

dorm room and scampered over to the library to make an important phone call.

It was nearly dark outside, but the early summer skies were still clinging on to the last scraps of light. The air was warm as I scrunched along the gravel path and pushed through the library doors.

Saint Smithen's library is one of my all-time favourite places. Firstly, it is full to bursting with shelves and shelves full of books that you can borrow whenever you like and you don't even have to pay anyone or anything. Secondly it is a really beautiful building full of cosy reading corners and a high ceiling painted with a mural of fat white clouds on a bright blue sky. It is also the home of the payphones that students can use to phone home and reassure their parents that they are brushing their teeth and wearing matching socks. I might not have parents in the traditional sense but it didn't mean that I had no one to call. Speaking to my circus family on the phone was always a great way to finish the day. (Not that they were really that bothered about the matching socks thing.)

In the Dougie Valentine books he writes all of the phone conversations out like a script and that's how I like to write mine as well because it means you can read them in all of the characters' voices. (And if someone is reading this book to you right now I hope you will make sure they really *commit* to their acting in this bit. That's a thing that Letty says when she wants you to act really hard, "*committing*".)

Here goes.

** Begin Transcript**

Cheery Baz: All right? Booming Badger 'ere.
Me: Cheery Baz! How are you?
Cheery Baz: (suspicious) Who is this?
Me: It's me, Poppy!
Cheery Baz: Oh.

Pause

Me: Soooo . . . how are things?
Cheery Baz: Things? All right, I suppose.
Me: Good, good.

Pause

Me: So . . . er . . . is there anyone else I can talk to? Is Pym around?
Cheery Baz: (shouting) OY PYM! IT'S WHAT'S

'ER FACE ON THE PHONE FOR YOU.

Scuffling noises

Pym: Hello, love! Sorry, was Cheery Baz talking your ear off as usual?!

Me: He seems even grumpier than normal.

Cheery Baz: (yelling in background) I CAN 'ear you lot, you know. And you'd be grumpy too if you 'ad to put up with snakes and lions all over the place.

Pym: No, he's only the usual amount of grumpy. *Lowers voice* But he *has* had another fight with Leaky Sue.

Cheery Baz: (shouting again) LEAKY SUE. Don't even mention 'er name in my presence. That dump that she calls an 'otel oughter be reported. Then she 'as the nerve to visit and say MY curtains clash with the cushions?! It's an OUTRAGE!

Fanella: (shouting in background) WHY IS ALL THIS SHOUTING? IS WAKING UP OTIS.

Cheery Baz: (grumbling) Should never 'ave let you bring that snake in 'ere in the first place.

22

Fanella: Bah. You sound just like Leaky Sue.
  You two are so the same is scary.

Cheery Baz: (grumbling noises in distance)

Scuffling noise

Fanella: TOMATO! Is you?

Me: Hi, Fanella.

Fanella: (hissing loudly) Tomato, I find
  something out. If you tell the Cheery Baz
  that he is acting like Leaky Sue he let
  you do whatever you want! Otis has his own
  room in the hotel now!

Cheery Baz: What's that you're saying?

Fanella: I SAY THAT YOU ARE HERO UNLIKE
  SILLY LEAKY SUE AND YOU RUN MUCH BETTER
  HOTEL.

Cheery Baz: Oh . . . all right then.

****Scuffling noise as phone is handed
  over****

Pym: Sorry for all the interruptions, Poppy.
  Tell us all your news.

Me: I wanted to let you know that we're

23

going on a school trip next week to the
seaside! To a place called Crumley Castle.

Pym: Well, that is very exciting! Crumley
Castle? That sounds familiar. . .

Fanella: You say seaside, Tomato? Make sure
you wear the suncream or you become real
life tomato! Ha! Is excellent joke. Also
beware for the sharks.

Pym: There aren't any. . .

Boris: (entering in background) Is someone
talking about sharks?! Where? Here?
Oh no! Is there going to be a shark
attack?!

Cheery Baz: There are NO sharks in this
establishment.

Fanella: Yes. Only the snakes and lions.
Silly Boris. Is Tomato is going to the
seaside and get eaten by shark.

Pym: THERE AREN'T ANY SHARKS. Poppy, I think
I have a guidebook for Crumley Castle
somewhere; we toured down that way years
ago. It has a very interesting history – I
think you'll be intrigued by some of the
mysteries! One in particular would be right
up your street. Shall I send the book over?

Me: Oooh, yes please, Pym! Is there really a mystery to solve?

Fanella: (thoughtfully) Maybe shark WOULD be good attraction for circus?

Cheery Baz: Now *that* is where I draw the line. I will NOT 'ave a shark in my 'otel.

Fanella: (sighs) Oh yes, just like Leaky Sue. Why you both hate nature so much, Cheery Baz?

Cheery Baz: (pause) Well. . . I suppose we could have some sort of tank out the back. . .

Pym: NO SHARKS! (sigh) Better go, Poppy.

Boris: We could call him Brian!

Enthusiastic agreeing noises

End of transcript

I hung up the phone with a chuckle. Talking to my family always made me feel better, and it helped to remind me that, whatever happened with Miss Susan, I had a family that loved and cared for me. I decided to try not to let things worry me so much, and to enjoy a trip to the seaside with my pals. I wondered what Pym's guidebook would reveal about Crumley Castle – and whether it might include another mystery ripe for solving by a certain trio of top detectives...

CHAPTER FOUR

A couple of days later Pym's guidebook turned up. Inside the parcel with the book was an old photograph of my circus family, taken long before I had arrived in their lives, all gathered outside what must be Crumley Castle. There was Pym standing next to Boris the strongman, whose head was covered in a mop of blonde hair. (I nearly didn't recognize him because I was so used to him being bald!) Tina and Tawna were doing handstands at one side, and Sharp-Eye Sheila was playing her banjo while Marvin, Doris, Chuckles and BoBo danced. Fanella was doing the splits across the front of the photo, and Luigi was holding a tiny

lion cub – baby Buttercup! Behind them was a castle that looked straight out of a fairy tale. It had a moat with swans gliding along inside it and there was a tall turret with a pointed roof sticking out from one side of the building. In front, the gardens were split on to lots of different levels, and even though the photo was a bit faded you could still see how bright and cheerful all the colourful flowers were, tumbling over each other. On the back of the photograph in smudged ink were the words "All of us at Crumley Castle" and underneath in fresh ink Pym had written, "Have a great time, Poppy! Hope these help! Pym xxx"

These? I realized then that there were two things in the parcel. One of the helpful things that Pym had sent was the guidebook, but the other helpful thing was ... a pencil sharpener. It might seem like a funny thing to send but the important thing is that Pym has visions, and if she gives you something that she tells you will be useful, no matter how random it seems, you know that it won't be long before it comes in handy. Sometimes it is a tissue before you sneeze or a torch before a power cut, and other times it is something more serious that comes in useful when you find yourself in a real scrape. I slipped the pencil sharpener in my pocket, and turned my attention to the guidebook.

There was a lot of interesting stuff about when the castle had been built and the family that lived there, but there was one section in particular that stopped me in my tracks. I have made a photocopy of the pages to stick in here for you to see yourself. (Obviously I would never rip out the real pages, because books deserve to be treated a lot better than that and should be regularly stroked and made to feel appreciated. You may like to do that with this one right now.)

CRUMLEY CASTLE – STEP INTO HISTORY!

If you are looking for history and a dash of mystery on your travels then look no further! Parts of Crumley Castle date back to the sixteenth century and there are plenty of eerie stories surrounding this ancient building – most spookily, the tale of the infamous Redshank brothers.

During the eighteenth century, Tom and Henry Redshank were fishermen who lived in Crumley village; but they were also notorious smugglers, often arriving onshore at the local beach (the aptly named "Smuggler's Cove") to unload their cargo of illegally obtained barrels of brandy. Their small sailboat, *Spinning Jenny*, had been painted black – right down to the sails – so that on moonlit evenings it was practically invisible to the naked eye. Tom would bring the illegal cargo by boat into Smuggler's Cove, and Henry would signal his brother that the coast was clear by lighting a lamp on the mainland and awaiting the answering "spark" from Tom.

The Redshanks were constantly on the run from

the law and one night, as they unloaded their cargo in the cove, they were ambushed by customs men. Furious gunfire was exchanged and while Tom managed to escape in the boat, Henry fled along the beach, only to vanish at the cliff face.

Eventually a scout alerted the officers that Henry Redshank had emerged inside Crumley Castle! The men sped up to the castle in hot pursuit.

Now, here's where things get really mysterious. The story goes that Henry barricaded himself in the castle's library, and apart from the door, which was locked from the inside and had men stationed outside, there was no way in or out. After about half an hour, the customs officers managed to break through the heavy door — and can you guess what they found? That's right. The smuggler had vanished into thin air! A thorough search of the room, from floor to ceiling, was undertaken — but no sign of Henry Redshank was ever seen again. Rumour has it that Tom escaped to the continent to start a new life, but what happened to his brother, nobody knows.

To this day, the mystery of Henry Redshank's disappearance has never been solved — a true smuggling legend for Smuggler's Cove!

Here was a mystery I could really get my teeth into. *Real life smugglers*! And not only smugglers, but *vanishing* smugglers! I couldn't wait to share the news with Kip and Ingrid – it looked as though our trip to Crumley Castle was going to be even more interesting than any of us had imagined. I wondered how the man had escaped from Crumley Castle and a locked room. Had Henry Redshank really just disappeared into thin air? When Kip, Ingrid and I joined forces I knew we were an unstoppable mystery-solving force – if anyone could unlock the secret of the smuggler's vanishing act, it was us.

CHAPTER FIVE

The next day I found myself and my well-stuffed backpack on the coach with a rabble of nineteen other thoroughly excited first years. Unfortunately, one of those nineteen other students was Annabelle Forthington-Smythe. (Or Annabelle Fartington-Smith as she is known in some circles.) Annabelle is the sort of mean girl who's used to getting her own way with everything. She *really* doesn't like me (even though I am totally charming and lovable all the time, except if you bend the pages in my favourite books when I can get a bit shouty). Annabelle was just about the only dark spot on this school trip and I had to admit I was a little bit worried about her. After all, Saint Smithen's was so massive we managed to avoid each other most of the time, but I feared that a camping site may be another story.

As Ingrid and I moved down the aisle of the bus, Annabelle followed behind, taking tiny sips from a half empty bottle of water. I slid into a window seat and Ingrid sat next to me. Suddenly, with a dramatic "Oh no!", Annabelle pretended to trip and flung her arm out towards Ingrid and me, the remaining contents of her water bottle splashing on the floor and in our laps. With a collective gasp we both jumped to our feet; fortunately Annabelle's aim was as terrible as her personality and there wasn't much damage done.

"What's going on?" asked Mr Grant from the front of the bus where he was checking off the register.

"Oh dear, Poppy, I'm SO sorry!" Annabelle batted her eyelashes at me. "What a terrible ACCIDENT." Behind her I heard one of her friends give a piggy little snort of laughter. It was a new girl called Barbie Gubbins who had turned into Annabelle's shadow. She even did her blonde hair in a bouncing ponytail like Annabelle's and bought matching clothes, so that they would look more alike. It made me feel sick – one Annabelle was more than enough, thank you.

"It's fine, Annabelle," I ground out, taking the tissue Ingrid offered me and dabbing at my lap. "We can't all have good coordination, can we? I'm sure it's difficult for you, being so clumsy." I smiled sweetly.

Annabelle smirked and carried on down to the back of the coach where she was quickly surrounded by her gaggle of annoying friends.

"Ugh. I hope she won't be like this for the whole trip," I said, closing my eyes.

"Don't worry," said Ingrid. "I'm sure they'll find something else to focus on."

At that moment Kip lumbered up the steps and on to the bus, bent double under the weight of the biggest backpack I have ever seen – easily the same size as him, maybe even a little bigger. (Admittedly, that's not so difficult. Kip likes to refer to himself as being a bit "vertically challenged".) He pushed his dark hair out of his eyes and looked around. Spotting me and Ingrid he yelled, "I see you! I'm coming! Hang on!" in his big voice and then, puffing with exertion, he started bashing his way up the coach aisle towards us, leaving a trail of battered and grumbling students in his wake.

"Oi! Watch it!" exclaimed one boy, rubbing his elbow.

"Oops! Sorry!" Kip apologized, turning to the boy and hitting another passenger right in the face as he did so.

"What have you got in there?" I hissed as he flung himself into the seat behind us, ignoring the dark grumblings of our fellow students.

"Just the essentials," Kip muttered, yanking the top of the bag open to reveal a HUGE stash of sweets and crisps.

"Have you packed any *clothes*?" Ingrid asked, leaning over the back of the seat to take a look.

"Er, yeah ... there are some in the bottom, I think," Kip replied before shoving an enormous gobstopper into his mouth, forcing him into a very uncharacteristic silence.

"So, Poppy – you've found us a mystery to keep us busy," Ingrid grinned, her eyes gleaming behind her thick glasses. "Do you really think we've got a chance at solving this puzzle of the smuggler's disappearance? After all, it has been hundreds of years..."

Kip began nodding his head vigorously and making gobstopper-filled mumbly noises. When I had revealed the information provided by Pym's guidebook it had taken absolutely no persuasion at all to get the two of them on board with the investigation. "I think we've solved more difficult mysteries!" I said, and Kip made some more mumbly gobstopper-filled noises in agreement. "We've had a lot of detective training by now . . . I reckon we stand a good chance. And I have some ideas already." I pulled out my notebook in which I had begun making case notes and flicked through the first couple of pages. "The first step will be to interview the owners of the castle, see if they have any ideas." I was interrupted here by more urgent mutterings from Kip, who had locked his hand around my arm in a frantic grip. ". . . Yes, yes, sorry, Kip," I said soothingly. "As agreed, the first step will be ice cream, but the *second* step will be interviewing the owners." Kip relaxed at this, and I pulled my arm to safety. "And then I think we need to investigate the so-called locked room for any other escape routes."

My team nodded encouragingly and I felt a wave of excitement wash over me. I never could resist a mystery – and if I was honest, it was nice having something to distract me from the even bigger, more secret mystery I needed to solve.

By this time the bus had started rumbling down the long school drive, away from Saint Smithen's and out on to the open road. The skies were clear and blue and the coach was already a bit stuffy. I pushed up the window and stuck my face out into the breeze like a happy dog. My skin was tingling with the feeling of adventure that a sunny day and a change of scenery often brings.

"Henry Redshank must have got from the beach to the castle somehow." Ingrid's voice reached my ears and I pulled my head back through the window so that I could listen. "But how ... that's what we need to find."

I nodded enthusiastically. "Yes, that's exactly what I thought," I said. "If we can find out how Harry Redshank got up to the castle in the first place, that might help us to work out what happened next."

We all fell silent, mulling over the potential mysteries that Crumley Castle and Smuggler's Cove might hold. My eyes wandered to the front of the bus, where Miss Susan was nodding and moving her hands as she chatted with Mr Grant in the seat next to her. Whatever she said made Mr Grant break into a short, rumbling laugh. As she turned her head towards him I caught a glimpse of her upturned mouth and smiling eyes.

I felt my heart squeeze in my chest, and from

somewhere far away I heard Ingrid asking if I was OK. I dragged my eyes away from Miss Susan and saw that Ingrid's face wore a worried frown. Kip's hand reached for my shoulder. I must have looked very odd indeed. I forced a smile.

"I'm fine," I said, my voice only betraying a slight tremble. "It's just a bit hot in here. It's making me feel a bit carsick," I added. Kip's hand was rapidly withdrawn, but Ingrid still looked worried. I had the feeling that over the last few months she knew there was something on my mind that I hadn't been telling her, but so far she hadn't pushed me to tell her what it was.

We were interrupted then, to my relief, by Mr Grant who threw his head back and began singing a noisy tune that involved lots of clapping and cheering at the right time. Everyone joined in enthusiastically, and the bus was filled with a rackety melody that almost drowned out Kip's terrible honking singing voice. (Kip has a lot of talents, but singing is just not one of them.)

After that the long journey passed uneventfully. There was some more singing and we managed to make a decent dent in Kip's confectionary collection. (Kip even won back some good feeling after the backpack debacle by offering an enormous bag of jelly worms around to everyone.) Eventually, we pulled off the busy main road and into a narrow, wiggling lane that was banked on either side by rambling hedgerows. We began winding our way along, holding our breath and hoping we wouldn't meet any cars coming the other way as the coach squeeeezed through, branches scraping along its sides. Then, all of a sudden we reached the top of a hill and the view opened up in front of us like a perfect postcard.

"The sea!" someone squealed, and we all cheered at the first sight of all that big, blue sparkling water, stretching right out to meet the sky. I held my face up to the window again and took a deep breath of salty air, cheering and hollering along with everyone else. The whole coach was humming with anticipation, as we waited for our very first glimpse of Crumley Castle . . . and suddenly, like something out of a dream, it appeared.

CHAPTER SIX

The castle was huddled on top of a cliff, like a big, dark monster, overlooking the golden curve of Smuggler's Cove and the shimmering blue sea. It had certainly not been well looked after in recent years, and it looked very different to the castle in Pym's photograph. The moat was empty and decidedly swan free, and the gardens at the front of the building were wild and overgrown. Some of the windows had boards over them, but all of these imperfections only seemed to add to the drama of the scene. Up close, Crumley Castle looked less like something from a fairy tale and more like something from a seriously spooky ghost story. Despite the clear blue skies, I almost expected to see forks of lightning strike the conical roof of the crooked turret, and to hear the rumble of thunder fill the air. The whole building practically crackled with adventure.

It was brilliant. And I could see that Kip and Ingrid felt the same as I did.

"Even if we didn't *know* there was a mystery here, we'd definitely suspect there was," I said excitedly, jumping down from the coach and on to the sweeping gravel driveway.

Ingrid was nodding. "It looks like somewhere a vampire would live," she said. Then, seeing Kip's horrified face, she quickly added, "In a story, I mean, not in real life, obviously. Because there's no such thing as vampires."

Kip was still looking a bit worried, so I chimed in as well. "We are going to have so much fun exploring this place!" I said. "There's going to be such a lot to see. . . Where do you think the kitchens are? They must be massive! Think how much cake there must be!" My food-related distraction tactics proved successful once more and Kip's eyes lit up in greedy anticipation, all thoughts of spooks and vampires banished in an instant.

We were interrupted then by the arrival of several people. A woman with gingery hair ran up to Miss

Susan and threw her arms around her. "Elaine!" she exclaimed.

"Agatha!" Miss Susan replied, returning her hug.

Behind Agatha was a tall, pale man. He had dark hair that was turning grey, and a sort of crumpled, worn-out look about him. He introduced himself as Agatha's husband, Bernard Booth. As well as the Booths there were two other men who had emerged from the castle at the sound of us spilling from the coach. A small man with thinning hair, and watery blue eyes behind thick glasses bustled forward. He was wearing a soup-stained cardigan and baggy brown corduroy trousers, and he smelled terribly musty. He began shaking Miss Susan's hand enthusiastically.

"How do you do?" he wheezed. "I'm Stanley Goodwill, a distant relation of Bernard's. Delighted to meet any friend of dear Agatha's. Delighted!" He was still shaking Miss Susan's hand and he kept repeating the word "Delighted!" while smiling vaguely at the huddled group of students in front of him.

"Stanley's been here for quite some time," Agatha explained. "He was living with Bernard's Great-aunt Ada before she passed away, so he knows the castle far better than us. He's a very respected historian, and he's writing a book on Crumley Castle." Stanley Goodwill rocked back on his heels and beamed around at everyone some more.

This news caught my attention. Perhaps this historian would have valuable information about the castle and the story of the vanishing Redshank brothers. We would have to try and get an interview with him at some point soon. I filed this away for discussion with Kip and Ingrid later on.

The man standing behind Stanley Goodwill was absolutely enormous – nearly as big as Boris the strongman. He was in his early twenties and his large, square head was shaved. A gold hoop earring sparkled in his left ear. Despite the heat he was wearing a very smart black suit over a black shirt. Poking out from under his sleeves I could just see the edges of tattoos on both arms. The man stayed silent and Agatha's voice shook a little as she introduced him. "And this is Horatio Muggins," she said, her hands fluttering in his direction. "He's... he's..."

"He's a friend of the family," Bernard said, finishing her sentence. And there was an awkward pause. "It's lovely to have you all here at Crumley Castle," Bernard eventually continued with a forced cheeriness.

By this point we were all getting a bit restless. Introductions were all well and good, but there was a *castle* and a *beach* to explore after all. There was only so long we could stay still with polite smiles smeared across our faces.

Luckily, Mr Grant seemed to know exactly what we were thinking. "Well, it's very nice to meet you all," he said, "but I think after that long journey this lot are ready to stretch their legs and do some exploring! Where do you want us?"

Agatha's hands fluttered by her sides again. "Of course, of course!" she cried. "Right this way, children." The men all disappeared back into the castle, Bernard Booth and Stanley Goodwill chatting easily and Horatio Muggins following silently behind.

Agatha led us along the front of the castle, and down some steps at the side into a large field that overlooked the sea. Laid out in neat rows were lots of white tents, trembling slightly in the salty breeze.

"You've put all the tents up already!" Mr Grant exclaimed. "Thank you! That must have been an awful lot of work."

"Fuddling did it." Agatha smiled a smile that was

like an especially weak cup of tea. "He's our butler – we inherited him with the castle. He used to be in the army, I think – anyway he's terribly efficient." She shrugged. "Now, over there" – she pointed in the direction of a long low building at the edge of the field – "we've converted one of the old stable blocks into bathrooms. You'll eat in the dining room in the castle itself, although there is a firepit down there" – she pointed towards the cliff edge – "if you want to have a campfire. Obviously we've put the fence along the edge there, but please do be careful, it's quite a drop."

"It's all looking so wonderful, Aggie!" Miss Susan said warmly.

Agatha smiled her weak tea smile. "Thank you!" she murmured. "We're a bit nervous, you know – it's such a big investment. So you must let me know how you get on. This is our trial run before we open up the campsite to the public, so any problems – no matter how small – must be ironed out."

Mr Grant turned to face us, a silver whistle hanging around his neck. "Right, you lot! Two to a tent, girls this side and boys over there. Drop your stuff off and get settled so that we can hit the beach!" There was a big cheer at this and everyone scrambled off.

Except me; I held back for a moment, listening hard in case Agatha and Miss Susan had anything revealing to say. It had occurred to me that the sort of conversation that took place between these old friends may prove useful in my investigation into Miss Susan.

"It's so good to see you, Aggie," Miss Susan said in a low voice, squeezing her friend's arm. "But where's Jenny?" she asked, looking back towards the castle. "I can't wait to see her; she must be so grown-up now!"

Agatha made a funny noise and then began to cough. A trembly hand tucked a strand of gingery hair behind her ear, but her voice was quite jolly when she said, "Yes, she's seventeen now, if you can believe it! But Jenny's away with some friends this week. I'm sure she's enjoying a break from us overbearing parents!"

That was the last I heard of their conversation, because Ingrid was tugging at my arm. "Come on, Poppy, or all the good spots will be taken!"

It didn't seem like Miss Susan and Agatha were about to have a chat about Miss Susan's long-lost secret baby anyway, and they began making their way towards the castle, so I allowed myself to be dragged off quite happily. The two of us secured an excellent spot near the steps to the castle and we dumped our backpacks in the tent. Inside were two purple foam mats and two neatly rolled red sleeping bags.

"This is so brilliant!" I said, clapping my hands together. "I can't believe we're camping together for a whole week!"

Just then the blasting of a whistle filled the air. Sticking my head out of the tent, I saw Mr Grant gathering the troops.

"Come on, Ingrid!" I cried. "It's time to get exploring!"

CHAPTER SEVEN

We wound our way in single file down the coastal path, which was rugged and twisty, cut into the side of the cliff, and the sound of the waves crashing against the shore rang out all around us. Near the bottom of the cliff we came to the village of Crumley itself. It was small but perfectly formed: a collection of buildings huddled around a tidy little village green. There was a pub called the Smuggler's Arms with a skull and crossbones flying outside, a tiny post office and convenience store, and a shop called Rita's Range that sold buckets and spades and postcards and nets for catching tiny crabs you might spot in rock pools. There were also three places of particular interest

to us: Stan's Plaice, the fish and chip shop; the Buttered Muffin bakery; and most importantly of all Honeybee's Ice Creamery. It was in front of this final establishment that our procession came to a screeching halt.

Mr Grant raised an eyebrow. "Oh, all right!" he said with a grin. "We are on holiday, after all. In you go." These were the magic words and we all flung ourselves through the doors, scrabbling for our spending money and crowding round the display that held dozens of tubs of ice cream. The two ladies behind the counter were scooping as fast as they could to keep up with the orders that were coming thick and fast. Beside me Kip was making a noise like a wounded animal.

"What's wrong?" I asked, looking him over to make sure none of his limbs had fallen off or anything.

"It's impossible!" he whimpered. "Look at all these flavours. . . How can I possibly decide?"

"We're here for a whole week," I said soothingly. "Don't forget, we can come back and try every flavour."

"You're right," Kip said seriously, his head tilted to one side as he squinted at the display. "Better have a system in place . . . don't want to miss any. I think I'll do them alphabetically."

We emerged moments later, Ingrid with a strawberry cone, me with butterscotch and chocolate sauce, and Kip, a double helping of banana and bubblegum flavour.

"Soooooo goooood," I mumbled, my mouth full.

The others made noises of agreement, as our procession towards the beach started up again. Slurping happily at the end of my ice cream I felt a wave of contentment washing over me. The sun was shining, we were on our holidays and I was eating ice cream with my best pals. There was even a mystery to solve, and I reminded myself that I needed to get cracking on some investigative research. As we rounded a final corner I realized we had reached the site of that very mystery . . . Smuggler's Cove!

Miles of golden beach stretched in front of me, and it was hard to believe that smuggling and gunfights had taken place here. I kicked off my flip-flops and joined the others in running and whooping across the sand, feeling it squish between my toes. Throwing myself forward I started turning cartwheels along the shoreline before sinking my feet into the cool water. Next to me Ingrid and Kip were both pink cheeked and wild-eyed. Most of the group, including Mr Grant, were in the water now. The wind whipped at my braids and we all waded further in, screeching and giggling.

"It's FREEEEEEEZING!" Kip hollered, the waves lapping around his knees, soaking the bottoms of his shorts.

"You wimp!" I cried, flicking water in his direction. That was all it took, and suddenly everyone was screaming, laughing, splashing each other in an epic water fight. Even Mr Grant joined in and it was really, especially excellent when we all banded together to completely soak him.

"All right, all right, I surrender!" he laughed, holding his hands up. "Let's sit in the sun and dry off a bit or it'll be a very soggy walk back to the castle."

We made our way over to some flat rocks that stretched out along the edge of the cove and into the water, and clambered up on top of them. The dark flinty grey stones had been smoothed by the sea and warmed by the sun, and they made the perfect spot to dry out. Squinting back over the beach I spotted Annabelle and Barbie and some of their pals. They had all wrinkled their noses up at the thought of getting their hair wet and so had plonked themselves down on the sand, their faces turned up towards the sun as they worked on their tans. They were talking to a tall man I couldn't see properly because of the sun. When Mr Grant noticed he waved cheerfully to the man and jogged over to them.

"Who's that?" I wondered aloud.

"Who?" asked Kip, propping himself up on his elbow.

"That man talking to Mr Grant." I pointed.

Ingrid shielded her eyes with her hand. "Looks like we're about to find out," she said, as Mr Grant and the stranger started walking towards us.

As they got closer I realized that the man with Mr Grant was younger than I had first thought, maybe about seventeen or eighteen. He was also very, very handsome with muscly arms and long bleached hair flopping into a pair of twinkly blue eyes. He had the sort of suntan that you only get from being outside all the time. *No wonder Annabelle was following along behind, twirling her blonde hair around her finger*, I thought with a roll of my eyes.

"Children!" Mr Grant called as he got closer, and

we all gathered around. "I want to introduce you to Jack Jenkins ... our surfing instructor!"

There was a ripple of excitement at this news, although I saw Ingrid's face fall a little bit.

"Surfing? Cool!" our friend Riley yelled, high-fiving the boy next to him.

Jack Jenkins smiled, showing off lots of straight, white teeth. "Hi, guys!" he said. "I'm excited to be working with you this week. We'll have you riding the waves in no time!"

There were more cheers and a crowd huddled around Jack, shouting out lots of questions about surfing. He laughed and began trying to answer them all. An older girl in a bikini came up and wound her arm around Jack's waist, whispering in his ear. "Be with you in a minute, Betsy-kins," he said in a soppy voice, giving her a starry-eyed smooch. With a smirk, Betsy wandered back to her friends, her hips swinging confidently. "Sorry about that!" Jack grinned. "The ladies love me!" He laughed and I struggled to control my need to eye-roll. The conversation turned back to surfing. When there was a lull I saw my opportunity.

"Do you know anything about the Redshank brothers?" I asked. Might as well see if this guy had any local gossip to add to our investigation, I thought.

Jack looked surprised. "The Redshank brothers?" he asked. "Sure, they're a bit of a local legend. They were famous smugglers," he explained to the rest of the group. "They used to live in Crumley and smuggle illegal goods right here in Smuggler's Cove. They were always having all sorts of adventures together, sailing around and getting into trouble, but no one could ever catch them – it was like they were untouchable. They actually sound like pretty cool guys – Henry Redshank was supposed to be the finest shot in the country and his brother Tom was an amazing swordsman." Jack's eyes lit up with enthusiasm, and he continued: "One night they were nearly caught and Henry just disappeared up at Crumley Castle, completely vanished from a locked room." He turned his head towards the shadowy presence of the castle, sitting imposingly on the top of the cliff.

"I read that the other brother, Tom, managed to escape too," I said quickly.

Jack nodded. "So the story goes. When the officers tried to pinch them on the beach right here, Tom left his brother behind and sailed off. Apparently he escaped to France and never came back to England, because they would have put him in prison ... or worse, but what happened to Henry..." Jack shrugged his shoulders here. "Nobody knows. It was all very mysterious, and actually pretty spooky." His eyes met mine and I felt a thrill of excitement as I realized there was more to the story.

"You see," Jack continued in a low voice, "the tale we were always told was that the brothers sold their souls through some sort of evil incantation and that's how they always managed to avoid getting caught, and how Henry vanished like that. People in the village said the brothers could walk through walls, and fly through the night cloaked in darkness. The reason no one ever saw Henry again was that he was whisked away to safety by the dark forces that lurk in the castle." All eyes swung back to the castle once more and Jack Jenkins shuddered as he added, "Some even say that he never truly left, and the restless ghost of Henry Redshank walks the hallways to this day, searching for the brother who abandoned him." He trailed off then, but catching sight of our nervous faces his toothy grin burst forth. "Don't look so worried," he said, and laughed, "they're only silly old stories."

I looked over his shoulder at the castle, that even with the sun shining seemed somehow sunk in shadows. Despite the warm weather a shiver snaked up and down my spine. Something spooky was definitely going on, and I had a feeling that the stories weren't silly at all.

CHAPTER EIGHT

Could it be true? Had Henry Redshank really used some kind of dark spell to escape from Crumley Castle that night? Was the place actually haunted? I turned this new information over in my mind, as we made our way back for dinner.

Obviously it was weighing on Kip and Ingrid as well, because after we had been walking in silence for a bit, Kip piped up in a super-casual but slightly squeaky voice, "So, what do you think about this incantation business then?"

"I think there's probably a more logical explanation for Henry Redshank's vanishing act," Ingrid said mildly.

There was another silence. "But, you know . . . the

castle *did* seem pretty spooky. We all said so when we first arrived," Kip said eventually.

I had to admit that this was true. Hearing Jack Jenkins talk about dark forces at work in the castle had made me feel all jittery, and Kip was right – I mean Crumley Castle was *exactly* what you would expect a haunted castle to look like, which was quite exciting apart from the bit where we had to sleep right next to it.

"I don't know," I said slowly. "I'm not sure if I believe in evil spells and things, but if there were going to be ghosts anywhere, I guess they'd be here." We had rounded a corner and now found ourselves back in the castle grounds, looking up at its hulking, shadowy bulk. I felt a stirring of butterflies in my belly. Even Ingrid looked uncertain, and Kip gulped loudly. "Still," I said, trying to keep my voice nice and cheerful, "I'm sure those stories are just made up. We should get on with the mystery – and prove there was nothing magical about Henry's disappearance!"

Kip gulped again. "Yeah," he said in his bravest voice. "No point getting scared by a silly story." Unfortunately for Kip at that moment a loud gong rang out, and he jumped in the air while making a very un-brave squeaking noise. Ingrid and I politely pretended not to notice.

"That must be them calling us in for dinner," Ingrid said and Kip looked pretty torn. I could see the internal battle written all over his face: on the one hand the castle was potentially haunted by the unhappy ghosts of a notorious smuggler. On the other hand, there would *be* dinner, and dinner might *even* include pudding. In the end there was no contest: the food won and Kip squared his shoulders before striding manfully towards the door to the castle.

As we joined the others in shuffling through the huge doorway I was full of excitement. Ghosts or no ghosts, it was thrilling to finally get a look inside Crumley Castle! It felt like a big moment as I gingerly stepped across the threshold, almost expecting a ghost smuggler to appear right there and then. He didn't, of course, and I peered around, trying to take in every detail.

On the other side of the huge door was a cool and slightly gloomy entrance hall. There was an enormous staircase reaching up from the middle of the room that split in two separate directions, and there were lots of closed doors that must lead off to the other rooms. The floor was made of big stone slabs and there were huge, faded rugs on either side of the staircase. On top of one of these rugs stood a table holding the gong that we had heard calling us in to dinner, and standing next to the gong was the man who must have rung it. He was an older man with a halo of white hair sticking out around his head, wearing a dark grey suit that had tails at the back and looked like it had seen better days. His face was all wrinkly, like a well-crumpled shirt, and he had a pair of gold-rimmed glasses perched on the edge of his nose, over which he was peering at us with obvious disapproval, when Agatha and Miss Susan entered from a door to the left.

"Ah, children!" said Agatha, "I see you've met our butler, Fuddling." She gestured to the man by the gong, who bent forward slightly at the waist, his face remaining stony. "Now, let me show you through to the dining room where you'll be having dinner courtesy of our housekeeper, Mrs Crockton." She guided us through a doorway on the right and we found ourselves in another huge room with a very high, beamed ceiling from which two dusty candelabras hung. Cobwebs clung to the frames, though someone had placed new white candles in them which were lit, sending shadows dancing around the room. Despite the fact I knew it was still light outside it felt much darker in here, as the small high windows didn't really give the sun a chance. There were two long tables stretching down the middle of the room, and the walls were hung with faded red-and-gold tapestries. We pulled out the heavy chairs and sat down, just as a door at the back of the room swung open to reveal Fuddling and a lady in an apron, who must be Mrs Crockton, carrying platters of food.

A hungry "Oooooh" went around the room, but was quickly cut short by the sight of the grey-coloured meat, over-boiled cabbage and under-boiled potatoes that appeared in front of us.

"Well, tuck in!" Mrs Crockton cried, beaming at us. "Oh, dear!" she exclaimed. "I've forgotten the gravy!"

I suppressed a groan. My stomach rumbled and my ice cream felt like it had been a long time ago, and I remembered Pym was always saying that sea air made you hungry.

Well, Kip must have been breathing an awful lot of air since we arrived, because he hoovered up everything that was put in front of him: the grey meat, the rock-hard potatoes, even the soggy cabbage. As Ingrid and I toyed with the food on our plate, Kip was looking around hopefully for seconds.

"How can you enjoy this?" I whispered, poking at something that might have once been a carrot.

"What?" Kip asked. "I'm hungry."

During dinner I had been keeping an eye on Miss Susan. She and Mr Grant weren't eating because all the grown-ups were going to eat together later on, but the two of them sat at the top of our table, drinking cups of tea and keeping an eye on us. It was strange seeing Miss Susan outside of Saint Smithen's. She seemed happy and relaxed, dressed in light trousers and a white T-shirt and talking to Mr Grant.

Suddenly she looked up and our eyes met. It felt like I had stuck my finger in an electric socket. Goosebumps rose all over my arms and I couldn't look away. Miss Susan frowned and turned to say something to Mr Grant before standing and making her way towards me. My mouth was dry as she approached and laid a cool hand on my shoulder.

"Poppy, can I have a word?" she asked.

CHAPTER NINE

Miss Susan led me through the entrance hall and into another big, though much more cosy, room. "This is Agatha's study," she said, and I admired the walls lined with shelves and shelves of lovely books. Miss Susan glanced around and gestured towards two armchairs. "Have a seat," she said. Taking a deep breath, I sat down and tried to avoid making eye contact with her. Looking into those green eyes that were a bit too much like mine made me feel too many things.

Miss Susan sat across from me and cleared her throat. A heavy silence hung in the air like a soggy blanket on a washing line. "So, Poppy," Miss Susan finally began, making me jump a little in my seat.

"I wanted to talk to you about your recent ... behaviour."

"My behaviour?" I echoed blankly.

"Yes." Miss Susan nodded. "You've been a bit distracted and distant in class, I've noticed, since I got back from my sabbatical – rather *jumpy*. I had hoped that a change of scenery may help with whatever problems you were having, but it seemed like, at dinner, you were... Well, I just wanted to see if everything was all right?"

My mind was buzzing. Miss Susan noticed me, she paid special attention to me – she seemed *worried* about me. Was this some sort of a maternal instinct? If she was the "E" who had left me at the circus then she must know I was her daughter – but she *didn't* know that *I* knew that. It was all a bit of a minefield.

Unfortunately, while I was riding this particular rollercoaster of emotion, Miss Susan was still looking at me. "Poppy, are you all right? Is there something you need to discuss?"

This could be the moment! I could confront Miss Susan right now, tell her that I knew the truth, and ask her all the questions bubbling away inside me.

Instead, I mumbled, "No, thanks. I'm fine ... just a bit tired." I just wasn't ready to have the conversation now. Once I asked the question I knew I wouldn't be able to take it back ... and I didn't know if I was ready to find out the whole truth just yet. What if I didn't like what I heard?

Miss Susan got to her feet. "OK, if you're sure," she said. "But if there is anything bothering you, you can come to me." Her pale cheeks went a bit pink. "I know I may not be your favourite teacher," she said quietly, "but I take my duties very seriously." With that she straightened her shoulders, and guided me out of the room and back to the dining room, which was full of noisy chatter and laughter.

Slipping back into my seat I noticed that the tables had been cleared and there was a piece of paper in front of me. "What's this?" I asked, picking it up.

"It's a map of the castle that Mr Grant just handed out," said Kip. "It shows you where we can go and where is off limits. We've got free time for the rest of the evening. What did Miss Susan want?"

"Oh, nothing," I said. "She was just checking in about some homework." I tried to keep the tremble out of my voice but I caught Kip and Ingrid exchanging concerned glances. "Really, I'm fine," I snapped, immediately feeling terrible at the shock on my pals' faces. Fortunately, just then, everyone started getting up to leave and so the moment passed.

"What shall we do now?" asked Ingrid brightly. "Is it time to get on with the investigation?"

"Yes!" I agreed enthusiastically, happy to focus on the mystery at hand. "And I think maybe we should start by talking to someone who knows this place pretty well!" I pointed to the back of the room where Mrs Crockton had just appeared through the swinging kitchen door once more.

With everyone else gone, the three of us edged over towards her. Mrs Crockton was busy laying one of the tables for the grown-ups' dinner, and I cleared my throat to let her know we were there.

"Oh, hello there!" Mrs Crockton exclaimed. "Is there something I can help you with?"

"We just wanted to say thank you for a lovely dinner," I said sweetly.

"Yes, it was all very ... special," Ingrid chimed in.

"Oh, aren't you little ducks," Mrs Crockton said, seeming pleased. "I'm still finishing up the other meal for the oldies. Would you like to come into the kitchen for a hot chocolate?"

"YES!" Kip pumped his fist in the air and barrelled after her into the kitchen. The three of us sat at a scrubbed wooden counter while Mrs Crockton bustled about, making three steaming mugs of cocoa with lots of squirty whipped cream on the top, that fortunately disguised the slightly burnt taste of the milk.

"Thank you!" we all chorused, slurping away noisily.

"Who's that?" Kip's voice suddenly piped up. He was pointing towards a silver picture frame on one of the kitchen shelves that held a photograph of the Booths smiling with their arms around a teenage girl with long, gingery hair.

"Ah!" Mrs Crockton's eyes softened. "That's Jenny, the Booths' daughter, a dear girl. She's seventeen and a bit of a handful, all right. Such a shame you couldn't all meet her. I think it would do her good having some young folk around this draughty old place, but I understand she's off visiting some friends this week. A last minute thing, I heard."

There was a pause and I cleared my

throat. "We were actually wondering if you knew anything about the Redshank brothers?" I asked. "We were learning about the history of the castle and heard about Henry Redshank's disappearance. It sounded like quite the mystery."

"Oh, it was that," Mrs Crockton said, nodding. "Vanishing from a locked room like that... It isn't natural."

"Do you know which room it was that Henry was trapped in?" I asked breathlessly.

"Not the exact one," Mrs Crockton replied. "Apparently it was the library – that's what all the records say anyway – but the castle doesn't have a library any more, though I suppose it would be Agatha's study."

"Oh, yes!" I exclaimed, having just recently been in there. "It's full of old bookcases." Mrs Crockton nodded again.

"Who was it who lived here when the Redshank brothers disappeared?" Ingrid asked keenly.

"Ahhh, well that would be Moira Booth," Mrs Crockton said with a smile.

"Moira Booth?" Ingrid murmured. "Like Agatha and Bernard Booth?"

"That's right," agreed Mrs Crockton, "Bernard's a distant relative. That's why he inherited the place when the last owner, his great-aunt Ada, died without any children."

"Oh yes, Agatha mentioned someone called Ada," I said beadily. "She said that Stanley Goodwill who we met earlier used to live here with her."

"Yes, he did," Mrs Crockton nodded again, "he came here to do some research on the castle years ago now, and he ended up staying and looking after her. Stanley was devoted to Ada, though I have no idea why. She was a real tyrant – very mean spirited and always stirring up trouble. Stanley was her second cousin once removed, or so he always says. I'm not sure what that means he is to Bernard . . . these family trees are very muddling."

I murmured in agreement. It was certainly difficult to keep track of everyone.

"But Stanley's so much a part of the furniture now, I don't think Agatha and Bernard could get rid of him even if they wanted to. He took Ada's death very hard, poor thing. He was with her right to the end."

"And when did the Booths – the new ones I mean – inherit Crumley Castle?" Ingrid asked.

Mrs Crockton pursed her lips. "Oooh. About six months ago, I reckon," she replied. "And a world of trouble it's brought them too. This draughty old place with everything broken and needing looking after. It'd be a weight around anyone's neck, this old money pit. Still, I suppose Ada left them her money so they've got the cash to invest in this new-fangled campsite, maybe that will turn things around."

"Couldn't they just sell it?" Kip asked. "A massive old castle like this must be worth a fortune!"

Mrs Crockton shook her head. "No they can't, more's the pity. The castle has been in the Booth family for generations and that's the way the inheritance is set up. If they want the castle and the money then they have to live here. If Agatha and Bernard don't want it then it goes to the next person in line. Not that anyone's ever had much luck living here. Something strange at work," she said again, her words hanging in the air.

"Do you live here in the castle as well?" I asked.

"Oh, no!" Mrs Crockton shuddered. "I live in the village. I couldn't live in the castle."

"Why not?" mumbled Kip, through a mouthful of whipped cream.

"Well, on account of the ghost, of course." Mrs Crockton waved a carrot peeler in our direction.

Kip went very still. "Mmmm," he said, and his voice was a bit squeaky. "We did hear something about that."

"The ghost of Henry Redshank, you mean?" I asked.

"Oh yes," Mrs Crockton carried on with her peeling, and carroty curls twirled from under her fingers. "Some say he vanished out of this castle as if by magic, but if you ask me, he never really left at all – leastways his soul didn't." She was gesturing with her carrot peeler again, punctuating her sentences with a jabbing movement.

"So, you really think there's a ghost here?" I asked. "Really, truly?"

Mrs Crockton turned to look right at me. "I don't think," she said in a low voice. "I *know*."

"You . . . know?" I whispered, excitement pulsing through me. "Do you mean. . ."

"That's right, dearie. I saw it with my own eyes . . . as clear as I see you sitting there. The ghost of Henry Redshank."

CHAPTER TEN

"You *saw* a ghost?!" All three of us burst out at once.

Mrs Crockton seemed very calm. "Yes," she said mildly. "I was standing right here in the kitchen looking through that open door." She pointed to the door that opened to the dining hall. "A shadowy man he was, and he vanished, right through that wall, just disappeared through it like it wasn't there." My eyes followed her pointing finger to the dining hall's stone wall. It certainly looked very sturdy. No human being could possibly pass through it.

I goggled at her as if *she* was a ghost.

"What did you do?" asked Ingrid.

"Were you scared?" Kip whispered.

Mrs Crockton smiled. "Well, I was a bit shocked

at the time, you understand – I dropped the pile of laundry I was holding all over the floor. But I always knew the place was haunted . . . and that I had 'the sight', just like me old granny."

"What's 'the sight'?" Kip asked urgently, looking nervously into Mrs Crockton's eyes.

She laughed. "Why, second sight, of course, the ability to see things other people can't . . . spirits and whatnot. But I didn't feel any threat from the ghost, you know. The air went a bit cooler just before he disappeared, but he didn't try to approach me or anything. There's no need to be afraid, ducks, not all ghosts are trying to hurt you. Some of them just have unfinished business, you see."

"And was it really Henry Redshank?" I asked, gripping the counter.

"It must have been," she said, turning to look staight in my eyes. "It makes sense that his spirit would be lurking in this house somewhere, after his brother abandoned him like that. Plenty of unfinished business there, I should think. Now, sorry, my lovelies, but I must get back to work. You run along and find something fun to do, but if you're ever after a chat or a biscuit you're welcome here!" She winked at us, and Kip at least looked slightly comforted.

The three of us left the kitchen, through the dining room and back into the entrance hall in silence.

"I can't believe it!" I finally exclaimed.

"I know!" honked Kip, gripping my arm fiercely. "There could be ghosts everywhere!"

We all glanced nervously around the room. "So, what do we do next?" Ingrid asked.

"We need to get a good look around Agatha's study," I said, "if that's where the smuggler's disappearance is supposed to have taken place."

"Do you still want to carry on?" Kip's eyes widened. "With the investigation, I mean. Now we know there's a real live ghost … or, rather, real DEAD ghost involved?!"

I shot him a steely look, even though inside I did feel rather nervous. "We're detectives, Kip," I said firmly. "We're *professionals*. We follow the clues wherever they lead. Like Dougie Valentine always says, 'A good detective must go where the evidence takes them… Now out of my way, you evil time-travelling alligator.'"

Kip swallowed, and then nodded. "OK," he said bravely, "you're right."

"We may have a problem, though," Ingrid muttered, looking down at a piece of paper in her hands. She turned it to show me and Kip – it was the map Mr Grant had given out at dinner. "Agatha's study is strictly off limits to us students."

I felt myself deflate. How frustrating! Of course, the place wasn't off limits to Miss Susan, and I had just been in there! If only I had known to be on the lookout for crucial clues. "We'll have to find a way in," I said quietly. "If we can't find a good excuse to get in there, we'll have to sneak in when it's not so busy."

We were interrupted then by the looming figure of Horatio Muggins appearing suddenly from the study in question. Kip let out a squawk of fear – the poor boy was obviously still on edge, but I had to admit that Horatio Muggins was a pretty scary-looking man. He smiled at us, a smile that didn't quite reach his eyes and that showed off a gold tooth, glittering to match his hoop earring.

"Hello, children," he rumbled. "I am Horatio Muggins . . . and you are?"

"Poppy," I squeaked, "and Kip and Ingrid," I said, pointing to my dumbstruck pals.

"And are you having a good time? Do you like the castle and the campsite?" he asked, much to my surprise.

"Er, yes, thank you," I said, cautiously. "It's really great . . . although the castle is a bit . . . spooky."

Horatio glanced around, a frown puckering his large forehead. "Yes. I see what you mean," he said. "It's all in need of a bit of a makeover."

"Well," I said a bit nervously, "I can't wait to start exploring."

He gave me a thoughtful look. "You should be careful, poking about in a crumbling old castle!" His dark eyes met mine. "We wouldn't want anyone to have an accident, would we?" With that he turned and stomped into the dining room, the ground practically trembling beneath his feet.

"Was it just me or did that sound like a threat?" I asked.

"It wasn't just you," Kip said as we made our way outside. "That guy is SCARY."

"Speaking of scary. . ." Ingrid muttered, and I groaned because coming towards us, with her blonde ponytail bouncing and a smug smile on her face, was Annabelle, and trailing in her wake was Barbie.

"Ugh. What are you losers up to?" Annabelle asked, looking at us as if we were something stuck to the bottom of her shoe. Barbie snickered as if

Annabelle had just told a completely hilarious joke.

"Nothing," I said quickly. "Just looking around. Why? What are *you* doing?"

"Miss Susan wants to see us," Annabelle said as she flounced past. "I expect she wants to give me the tour of the place." She smirked and tossed her blonde hair over her shoulder. "After all, I am something of a VIP."

"What's a VIP?" Barbie asked, gormlessly.

"A very important person, of course," Annabelle snapped.

"Oh." Barbie's eyes were shining as she stared worshipfully at Annabelle. "Then yes, you are," she said. "A VVVIP."

Annabelle smiled at Barbie, as if looking at her was an enormous favour. Barbie practically swooned and I shook my head. "Well, we'd better go. Leave you three little kids to your games," Annabelle said, and with that, she skipped up the steps and disappeared further into the castle for a cosy chat with the woman who was also secretly my mother.

I felt something twist inside me. Miss Susan and Annabelle always seemed to be pretty chummy.

It was one of the things that had made me dislike the chemistry teacher so much in the first place, but now it felt like a real betrayal. How could Miss Susan like Annabelle? Didn't she care that she was so mean to me? I tried to pay attention to Kip and Ingrid's conversation, but anger was whistling inside me like a hot kettle coming to the boil.

We made our way back through the grounds to the campsite. It was getting dark now, and students were drifting down to the roaring firepit to tell ghost stories and toast marshmallows. I felt like I had had enough of ghosts for one day, but I was never one to turn down a marshmallow (and, as you can probably guess, neither was Kip), so we wandered down to join them. The firepit that Agatha had pointed out earlier was going great guns now, and the view out over the sea was pretty spectacular. Fortunately, the Booths had erected a sturdy wire fence along the edge of the cliff. Peeking through the holes, I felt my knees go all wibbly at the sight of the drop down the sheer cliff face.

Snuggled by the fire, underneath the twinkling stars, I forgot about all the mysteries swirling in my head for a while, happy to listen to ghoulish tales of severed heads and unspeakable curses that destroyed all cakes for ever (can you guess whose horror story that was?!). Eventually, Mr Grant told us it was time to brush our teeth and get into bed, and I for one was very relieved to snuggle down inside my sleeping bag.

I went over the day in my head. A lot had happened, and it seemed as though the mystery of Henry Redshank's disappearance was taking a decidedly spooky turn. With a yawn, I turned over the question of getting into the old library in my mind, but my brain was definitely too sleepy for devious plan-making after such a long day. I felt my heavy eyelids closing. . .

It seemed like only seconds later that I woke up, confused for a moment by the darkest of darkness that wrapped itself around me before I remembered where I was. Everything was quiet, apart from the distant hooting of a lonely owl. Squirming about in my sleeping bag, the tent felt warm and stuffy so I decided to have a look around outside and get some fresh air. I grabbed my torch before opening the zip at the front of the tent as quietly as possible, trying not to disturb a gently snoring Ingrid.

Shining my torch on my watch I saw that it was just after midnight. I trained the light on the ground and made my way towards the front of the field where I could hear the sound of the waves lapping against the shore below. My eyes had adjusted to the darkness now and I turned my torch off so as not to disturb any nature that may be around. I wondered if I might spot an owl or a fox.

It was at that particular moment that I spotted instead something so unexpected that it left me frozen to the spot, an icy feeling of dread trickling through my veins. With a gasp I forced my feet to move one in front of the other until I was stumbling back to the tent as fast as my legs would carry me. Sticking my head through the front of the tent I hissed, "Ingrid! Ingrid!"

"Mmmmm? Bacon and eggs please, Dad..." Ingrid murmured sleepily.

"I'm not your dad, Ingrid! Get out here NOW." The urgency in my voice must have woken Ingrid up properly because she sat bolt upright and then squirmed her way out of the tent towards me.

"What's the matter?" she whispered, and I could feel her trembling beside me. Without another word I took her arm and guided her gently in the direction I had come from. When we reached the cliff edge I pointed out towards the sea. Ingrid stiffened. "Is that—" she began, but I turned her to face the castle. She gasped.

Up in the turret window a light was burning. And out on the water a blue light was flashing in response. I felt a wave of excitement crash over me.

"I can't believe it," Ingrid whispered. "Is that ... *smugglers*?"

"I don't know!" I hissed, "but that was definitely what was described in the book about how smugglers communicated: a light on the mainland and a light out at sea, I didn't even think there *were* smugglers any more."

There was a pause. "You don't think..." Ingrid trailed off in a quavering voice.

"What?" I asked.

"Well, you know, what Mrs Crockton said ... about the ghost."

I let out a low whistle. "Ghost smugglers? That would really be something!"

And then, both lights went out.

CHAPTER ELEVEN

The next day we filled Kip in over breakfast. "Ghost...
Smugglers..." he repeated slowly. "As in ... *the ghost of
an evil dead smuggler who is in this castle*?" He gestured
around the dining hall. Ingrid and I both nodded.
"Wow ... great. Great. That's totally..." Kip trailed off.

"Great?" I suggested.

"Yup, yup." Kip nodded. "Ghost smugglers. No
big deal, right. I mean we've handled worse than
that. It's ... great." His voice was getting higher and
higher which led me to believe that he did not find
this news "great" at all.

"We don't *know* that it was ghost smugglers,"
I pointed out. "It could have just been ... real
smugglers."

"Mmmmm." Kip agreed, slurping on his orange juice. "*Much* better. Just illegal smugglers creeping around at night. Great." Again, I didn't get the sense that Kip thought this was great news at all.

"Well, I think if the light was on in the castle we should probably ask the Booths about it," I said, putting into words a thought that had been rolling around my head all morning. "After all, there may be some sort of simple explanation. And the other light at sea could have been a coincidence – we don't know for sure that the lights were signalling each other."

"Hmm," Ingrid said, pushing her glasses up her nose. "Two unrelated lights both going off at the same time?"

"Well," I said, "we should talk to them, even if it's to rule out the possibility." That was another rule of detecting; never ignore the most obvious solution – even if it's a bit boring.

Agatha and Bernard were also in the dining room, eating toast and talking to Miss Susan. I pushed my chair back and stood up. "No time like the present!" I said cheerfully. The three of us made our way over.

"Good morning, Poppy," Miss Susan said, in her cool voice. "Agatha, Bernard – this is Poppy and her friends Kip and Ingrid." The Booths looked very tired and crumpled and they both gave us slightly forced smiles. "Is there something I can help you with?" Miss Susan asked.

"Actually," I said nervously, "we had a question for Mr and Mrs Booth." Miss Susan's eyebrows raised slightly at this, but I ploughed on. "I just wondered whose room was up in the turret?" I asked.

Agatha and Bernard looked surprised. "Why, no one has the room in the turret," Bernard said, "it's been boarded up for years. Apparently the stairway is unstable." He rubbed his face with his hands. "Another problem with this old building."

"But – but I saw a light in there last night!" I blurted out, and then immediately regretted it.

Now the Booths looked *really* surprised.

"But no one has been up there for years!" cried Agatha. "It's certainly been boarded up since before we arrived, and Stanley said he'd never seen it open either."

"You must have been mistaken, Poppy," Miss Susan said, looking anxiously at her agitated friends.

"I'm not!" I exclaimed hotly. "Ingrid saw it too."

"Is this true?" Miss Susan turned to Ingrid.

"Yes, miss." Ingrid nodded. "Definitely."

"Oh, Elaine." Agatha was twisting her hands now and fidgeting in her seat. "You don't think one of the students got up there, do you? It's dangerous!"

"I'm sure it's all a misunderstanding, darling," her husband said soothingly. "In fact – why don't we just go and have a look?"

"That's a good idea," Miss Susan agreed. "I'm sure there's a simple explanation."

Agatha and Bernard began leading the way and me, Kip and Ingrid fell in behind Miss Susan. No one told us we *couldn't* come along, so we stayed quiet, not drawing attention to ourselves. We began zigzagging our way down a long corridor. I noticed that the further away from the main rooms we got, the shabbier the castle looked. The smell of damp filled the air.

On our journey we ran into Stanley Goodwill and Horatio Muggins, who were both coming the other way. "What are you lot up to?" Horatio asked, glowering at us from under his brows. Stanley, who was wearing the same crumpled cardigan and baggy trousers as the day before, rocked back and forth on his heels, humming a tune and smiling his vague smile.

"Oh, nothing, nothing," Agatha fluttered nervously.

"We're just checking that the turret is boarded up safely."

"And why do you need to do that?" said Horatio, his voice a low rumble of thunder. Agatha seemed to choke back a nervous sob.

"Because it's a health and safety risk," Miss Susan said frostily. "Why? Is there some sorrrrrrt of prrrrroblem?"

Even Horatio Muggins was no match for Miss Susan at her high-and-mightiest, when her voice got a bit frilly. "No, no," he grunted, holding his hands in the air. "We're off for breakfast, anyway. Come on, Stan." And with that he pushed past us.

"Ah, yes." Stanley's watery blue eyes focused on us and he smiled again. "Breakfast, eh? Delighted! Delighted!" He tottered off after Horatio. "Oh!" he exclaimed, looking back over his shoulder, "Agatha, I hope you won't mind if I do some work in your study this afternoon?"

"No, of course not, Stanley," Agatha said weakly, summoning a trembly smile. "You know you don't need to ask."

"Dear girl," I heard Stanley say to Horatio Muggins who made a sort of non-committal grunting sound in response.

"Come on," said Bernard with a sigh, drawing our attention back to the matter in hand. "Let's just get this over with." We walked further along the corridor taking a left and then a right, Bernard clicking light switches on as we went so that the light bulbs buzzed slowly to life. Rounding another corner, we came to a large doorway. Or it would have been a doorway if you could have seen it underneath all the wooden boards, the DANGER: KEEP OUT signs, the yellow-and-black stripy tape, and the chains and huge old padlock. It was very clear that no one could get in or out of this door even if they wanted to.

"Here we are – and it's locked," said Bernard unnecessarily. "There's no way anyone was in there last night."

I peered closely at the door. It was obvious from the dust coating everything that nothing had been touched for a long time, and there was not so much as one loose board that could have been prised away.

"And there's no other way in?" I asked.

"No, that's the only way," Agatha replied looking relieved. "Well. Thank goodness that's not one more thing to worry about."

"It was just a mistake," said Miss Susan. "I'm sure

Poppy didn't *mean* to make you anxious." She shot me a flinty look.

"No, but—" I began.

"Good. Then that's settled. You and Ingrid must have been confused. Now let's get back to our breakfasts." Miss Susan gently nudged Agatha and Bernard ahead of her.

Kip, Ingrid and I hung back slightly, looking confusedly at the door to the turret.

"Are you sure no one could get in that way?" Kip asked. "Even picking the lock or using some of your tricks?"

I shook my head. "Even if they had, it would be obvious because the dust would be disturbed. No – no one's been near that door in months, maybe years." Kip and Ingrid both looked as puzzled as I felt.

"But if that's true," Ingrid said slowly, "Then who – or *what* – lit the lamp up there last night?"

CHAPTER TWELVE

As hard as it was to believe, it was beginning to look as though the presence of a ghost was a real possibility – first Mrs Crockton, who had actually seen a ghost, and now the inexplicable light in the turret.

I wondered what Dougie Valentine might do in this situation and the answer came to me in a flash of brilliance. He would dig deeper of course, gather more information.

"We need to find out more about the Redshank brothers," I said to Kip and Ingrid later that afternoon, after we had come back from a big nature walk led by Mr Grant. "And I have an idea how. . ."

"I've been thinking the same thing," Ingrid said,

"but we're not at Saint Smithen's; we can't just nip to the library. The only one here is off limits." I could tell her voice that she was really pining for the well-organized shelves of the school library.

"No," I said gleefully, "but we *can* ask an expert! An expert on Crumley Castle to be exact."

When they looked blank I said, "Stanley Goodwill! An actual historian studying Crumley, under our roof – he'll have all the answers."

"Of course," breathed Ingrid. "Great idea, Poppy."

I dusted my fingernails on my T-shirt. It *was* a pretty great idea, I had to admit.

"And even better, he said he'd be working in Agatha's study," I said. "Let's go and see if he's there now... Maybe we can even have a quick look around the room if he invites us in!" It was the best plan we had, and we also had an hour to kill before Mr Grant took us rock climbing, so it seemed worth a shot.

When I knocked tentatively on the door there was a pause, then Stanley opened the door and peered out at us from behind his thick glasses. He had ink on his hands and his thin hair was rumpled.

"Yes?" he said, expectantly.

"We're sorry to bother you, Mr Goodwill," I said in my politest voice. "We know that you're a historian, and that you're working on a book about Crumley Castle, you see. We had some questions ... about the Redshank brothers."

"Ahhh!" He wheezed happily. "Questions – I adore questions! Come in, come in!" He stood back and gestured for us to come and sit down. I turned and grinned a victorious grin over my shoulder at Kip and Ingrid. We were in! "I was just making some notes," he said, running his hand distractedly through his hair and setting it even more on end. "Let me move these things out the way," and he began lifting pages and pages of notes from the various seats and surfaces around the room.

I cast my eye beadily around the room this time, paying much more attention than I had during my last visit. As well as a very old-looking desk and a pretty fireplace I noticed the painting hanging over the mantelpiece.

"I see you've spotted the portrait of Moira Booth!" Stanley exclaimed. "This was in her younger days of course... Quite the beauty, eh?"

The painting was of a young woman, about eighteen years old. Her chestnut hair was piled on top of her head and coiling over one

shoulder, a green ribbon threaded through it. She wore a fancy green dress edged in pale lace, and had delicate pale skin and flushed pink cheeks. The thing you really noticed first, though, were her eyes, which seemed to look straight at you from out of the painting, and even though her mouth wasn't exactly smiling there was something twinkly and mischievous in her eyes that made her look like she was about to burst out laughing. I liked her face immediately.

"Fascinating woman, Moira Booth," Stanley said,

turning and peering at me through his enormous glasses. "Oh yes, she was *quite* the character as I understand it."

I looked back at the portrait of the lady in question. "She looks like someone you'd want to be friends with," I said.

"Moira played an important part in the story of the Redshank brothers and Henry's disappearance, you know." Stanley bobbed his head up and down like a nodding dog.

"Did she?" I asked quickly, and I saw Kip and Ingrid perk up as well. That was news to us. So far no one had mentioned Moira Booth's involvement at all. "Mrs Crockton did say that she owned the castle at the time," I said thoughtfully, "but not that she had anything to do with the ... events of that particular evening."

"Anything to do with them?" Stanley repeated with a wheezy chuckle. "Why, she was the only witness as to what went on in this very room!"

"She saw it?!" Kip, Ingrid and I all exclaimed in one big voice.

"Well, as to that, we don't know exactly what she saw..." Stanley said mysteriously. "But not much, I would imagine."

He caught sight of our puzzled faces.

"If you're interested in the story then there's a fascinating account here..." Stanley began bustling around the room, looking for something. I took this opportunity to peer around some more, and I noticed that Kip and Ingrid were doing the same. My attention was captured by a long green tapestry that hung over a wall between the bookcases; it was similar to the ones in the dining room, but prettier, covered in a design of golden flowers.

"Now where is it?" Stanley muttered to himself, running his finger along the bookshelves. "Ah, here we are!" he exclaimed, holding a thin and very old-looking leather-bound book in his hand. "Now, I think you'll find this very interesting. Moira Booth was quite the progressive mistress of the castle, and she taught all her servants to read and write – quite unheard of at the time, you know. Anyway" – he waved the book gently – "this is Mrs Bidders's diary; she was the cook here at the time. It's mostly keeping inventory and notes about the kitchen, but her account of Henry Redshank's disappearance is rather fascinating reading. I'm sure Agatha won't mind if you borrow it to have a read – as long as you're very careful."

"Oh, we will be," breathed Ingrid, taking the book that Stanley offered her and stroking its cover reverently.

"What do *you* think happened to Henry?" I asked. "Do you believe the ghost stories?"

Stanley sighed. "I don't know, my dear," he said. "I didn't used to believe in ghosts, but being here . . . you see things. Things that can't be explained. . ." He trailed off.

"What sort of things?" Kip asked quickly.

"Oh, all sorts," he said with a shrug. "Strange shadows, things moving from the place you left them, odd lights and noises. Ada used to say that as long as they left you alone, you should just let them get on with their business."

"I forgot that you were here before the Booths arrived!" I exclaimed. "What was Ada Booth like?"

"She was a dear, dear lady!" Stanley exclaimed, his watery eyes looking even waterier than usual. "Very frail of course, by the end, but she was always so kind to me." He pulled out a large hanky and blew his nose. "I came here years ago to do some research on the castle. This book has been my life's work, you see. Ada took me in, asked me to stay and keep her company. Well," he said, gesturing around the room, "it's a big place to rattle around in by yourself. It's such a shame that dear Bernard and Agatha never met her, I'm sure they'd have loved her. They're such a kind couple, letting an old duffer like me stay – but, of course, this is the only home I have." His eyes got misty here, and he dabbed at them with his hanky. "And it's such a special place," his eyes swept adoringly around the room, "a real historical marvel." His face looked quite fierce suddenly, as though he thought we were about to disagree with him, but the look quickly vanished to be replaced by his usual absent-minded smile. "Now, if you don't mind, I had better get back to work. You let me know when you've had a chance to read the book."

"We will! Thank you!" the three of us chorused, and we scuttled out of there as fast as we could. I couldn't wait to get stuck into the book that Ingrid was clutching like a precious jewel. Who knew what clues the diary might hold, and what secrets it may reveal about the ghostly smugglers?

CHAPTER THIRTEEN

We found a quiet spot in the grounds, underneath an oak tree that provided some welcome shade on another sunny day, and settled down on the warm grass. Ingrid leafed gently through the book until she found the right pages. The handwriting was messy, the spelling was pretty terrible and the ink was very splotchy, but the cook's story made for very interesting reading.

5th June 1747

Wot a scene we have had in the castle this nite! Young Henry Redshank has dissap diserp dis vanished away somewhere, tho the good Lord knows where, and I pray for his eternal sole.

I were getting on with me usual chores, when I made me way from the kitchen to the liberry to ask Mistress Moira if there were ennything else she needed before I turned in, and rite there in the entrance hall I near enuff bumped into one of them Redshank lads all muffled up in dark scarves with his hat pulled low, but there was no mistakin the murder in those eyes. So I scream and one of them customs lads comes running in and starts yelling at the boy ter drop his weapon. Well, it seems ter me this only reminded the boy that he had a pistol, and he pulled it out mighty cool before he began backing up. He had nowhere to go but towards the liberry door. "NO!" I cried out. "Miss Moira's inside!" because the liberry was where she liked to do her reading and whatnot of an evening.

The Redshank lad — Henry I'm sure it was, though it was terruble hard to say with him all bundled up — stepped inside the liberry and closed the door with an awful click that meant it was locked.

"What is the meaning of this?" I heard me poor mistress cry, and my heart near burst at the fear in her voice.

"Just get down and stay quiet, or I'll make sure you regret it," I heard Henry growl in a low, hoarse voice. And then there were the sound of thumpin and bangin and Mistress Moira was shrieking in fear. I could hear the officers all hollering up the path. I for one thort they couldn't arrive soon enuff.

"He's locked himself in the liberry with my poor mistress," I cried.

So the officers start shouting to come out with your hands up, but there's no reply from the Redshank boy and so they start smashing down the door and the whole time Mistress don't say a word and I were so ~~ank ankshus anx~~ worried.

But when the door finally broke open, bless my sole if that boy hadn't completely vanished into thin air. And there on the floor, pail and unconscious was poor, dear Miss Moira, and I rushed over to her.

I have never known her take so weak before, not even when poor old Bill near chopped his thumb clean off. And I was trying to find some smelling salts to put under my mistresses nose, when she squeezed my

hand and said, "It's all right Sally, I'm quite well."
I helped her up to her feet and she were very pail
but also very dignerfied. Even though the room were
terrible warm the poor dear were shivering in her
nightgown and I wrapped her in a blanket and took
her over by the fire (which were smoking something
awful — I will be havin words with Bill about that
chimbley).

"But where is he?" my mistress finally managed
to whisper, looking about her. "Did you catch the
man?" And her voice were weak as a kitten and
enough to break yer heart.

But there was no sign of the Redshank boy and
those men checked all the windows (tho I new they
had been sealed shut these many years) and turned
the room upside down. And wot dark magic had
been at work I don't know, but there was no way in
or out of that room except for walking right past
us all and that he never did. They pulled that room
apart for hours but it was no good. The Redshank
boy were gone and I do not know but the work of
the divil himself has been here.

For a second we were stunned silent, and there was not a sound but the breeze rustling through the trees overhead. "Is there anything else?" I asked breathlessly, my voice just a little too loud.

Ingrid flicked through the remaining pages. "No, nothing about Henry Redshank."

"Poor Moira!" I exclaimed. "Although, what an adventure! She really was the only witness."

"But an unconscious one," Kip pointed out. "We still don't know *how* Henry disappeared, and it doesn't sound like Moira did either."

"I've been thinking," I said after a moment, "that maybe I should ask my family if they have any ideas about Henry's disappearing act. I mean, it sounds like the sort of magic trick Doris would think up."

Kip and Ingrid both nodded. "That's a great idea," Kip said. "Especially because it wouldn't involve a single ghost!"

Our conversation was interrupted then by the sound of raised voices approaching. Peeking around the tree trunk I saw that Agatha and Bernard Booth were approaching and it looked like they were having a heated argument. Putting my finger to my lips, I signalled to Kip and Ingrid to stay quiet.

"We have to go to the police!" Agatha was saying,

in a loud, trembling voice. She sounded close to tears. "How long can we let this go on without doing anything?"

"You know we can't do that!" Bernard snapped back as they came to a stop on the other side of the tree. "It could be the very worst thing to do. What if someone gets hurt?"

"But, Bernard. . ." Agatha was sobbing now. "This is just terrible, terrible. Where will we get the money?"

"I don't know. . ." Bernard's voice trailed off miserably.

"I hate this place, Bernard!" Agatha cried. "There's something wicked at work here. There's been nothing but one disaster after another since we arrived, and now this – the unthinkable – has happened."

"Hush!" Bernard cut her off suddenly. "Here comes Fuddling. Don't let him see you upset." There was a snuffling noise as Agatha tried to pull herself together. Fuddling was coming towards us and the three of us shuffled around to the side of the big tree as fast as possible. We were now stuck between Fuddling and the Booths, and I held my breath for fear of discovery.

"Ahh, Fuddling!" Bernard said in a completely different, big cheerful voice. "Anything the matter?"

"No, sir," came the monotone reply. I realized I hadn't heard Fuddling speak yet, and his voice was very dry and unemotional. "Mrs Crockton would like a word with Mrs Booth about the children's dinner. Whenever it is convenient," he continued.

"Fine, fine!" Bernard said. "We'll both go, shall we, love?" and I heard Agatha make a muffled noise of agreement before they turned to wander back towards the castle.

I waited a second before cautiously peeking back around the tree. To my surprise Fuddling was still standing there frozen to the spot, and a shiver rippled through me like raspberry sauce through ice cream when I caught a glimpse of his face.

As he watched the Booths walk off together his eyes followed them, and in those eyes was a look of pure and unadulterated hatred.

CHAPTER FOURTEEN

"What was all that about?" Ingrid gasped, after Fuddling left and I gave the all-clear.

"I don't know, you guys," I said slowly. "But you should have seen the look on Fuddling's face as the Booths walked away . ... it was like he hated them. I mean, *really* hated them."

"And what about all that stuff the Booths were saying about the police?" Kip muttered. "And getting hold of some money. What do you think is going on there?"

"I don't know," I said again, "but it sounded pretty serious, whatever it is." Were the Booths in some kind of trouble? I wondered. And if so why couldn't they go to the police? Perhaps they were on the wrong side of the law, just like the smugglers. It was all so confusing, and there were so many unanswered questions. I had been full of confidence before we began to tackle this mystery, but the further into it we got, the more questions there seemed to be.

"I think tonight we should keep watch and see if the lights come on again," I said at last. "I don't know what's going on with the Booths or if it's related to the smugglers, but this is the biggest lead we have."

Ingrid nodded, but Kip looked less convinced. "But. . . What if it's a ghost?" he said in a low voice.

"I definitely think there is a human hand at work here," I said with slightly more conviction than I felt. "But if it *is* a ghost then . . . I don't know, maybe we can ask *him* what he's up to."

Kip looked at me like I had sprouted a second head, but I knew that we were going to have to do *something* drastic if we wanted to solve this mystery. It was time to take action.

Our plan may have had to wait until the evening but that didn't mean the rest of the day was going to waste. After our rock-climbing lesson with Mr Grant, which I, for one, really enjoyed (Ingrid, on the other hand, definitely did not), we moseyed into the village to sample the wares of the Buttered Muffin bakery and Kip continued his ice cream alphabet odyssey (Ingrid and I were only too happy to offer our assistance with this). We were in the bakery, paying for our warm saffron buns when Mrs Crockton bustled in with a big wicker basket over her arm.

"Oh, hello again." She smiled. "I hope I didn't scare you too much with all that ghost talk yesterday."

"No, no," I said reassuringly. "We were really, really interested. We all think the story of the Redshank brothers is completely brilliant."

"Well, it's certainly a fascinating slice of history." Mrs Crockton smiled again as she began filling her basket with crusty loaves of bread.

"Yes, Mr Goodwill let us borrow a book all about it. It was written by Moira Booth's cook," Ingrid piped up.

"Oh, really?" Mrs Crockton looked surprised. "I had no idea that existed. Well, now you three know more about it than I do!"

"It sounds really spooky," I said. "No one seems to know how Henry Redshank escaped."

"Unless there really was a dark spell involved." Kip shuddered.

"You don't really believe that do you?" Ingrid asked.

"Mrs Crockton did see a ghost!" Kip reminded us, and Mrs Crockton nodded. "Clear as I see you and me," she said. "Though it's nice to hear someone believes me. Old Fuddling never believed that I had seen that ghost, even though I swore up and down that I had."

"Mmmm." I nodded, sensing my opportunity. "But," I said carefully, "he does seem a bit ... grumpy."

Mrs Crockton laughed at that. "Well, that's a polite way of putting it, duck, but you're quite right – the man's a misery guts and no mistake."

"Is he upset about anything in particular?" Ingrid asked, innocently.

"Well, he always was a grumpy so-and-so," Mrs Crockton raised her eyebrows, "but he's been unbearable since Agatha and Bernard arrived."

"Why?" I asked quickly. "Doesn't he like them?"

"Oh, now I wouldn't say that." Mrs Crockton shook her head hastily. "I think he's just disappointed. Old Ada Booth – Bernard's great-aunt who left them the castle – well, she always made out like she was going to leave Fuddling a bit

110

of money, see? Enough to retire on at least. But she didn't leave anyone a penny except Bernard – he got the lot."

"Well, that must have been very upsetting," I said.

"Fuddling was daft for believing her," Mrs Crockton said firmly. "Everyone knows old Ada used to promise everyone she'd be leaving 'em money one of these days. Loved stirring up trouble, she did, and making everyone bend over backwards to stay on her good side. Used to say the same to me, not that I ever paid a bit of attention to her, the old goat." Mrs Crockton was distracted then by the need to pay the man behind the counter. When she had finished she turned back to us, "Now, look at the time!" she exclaimed. "What a gossip I am! I'd better be getting back and making your dinner. Don't fill up on saffron buns too much, will you?" She gave us a wink and disappeared out the shop and up the path to the castle.

Leaving the bakery, we called in to Rita's Range to buy postcards and stamps. I wanted to send one to the circus and fill them in on our adventures and I chose a postcard with a picture of Smuggler's Cove on the front. I also bought a packet of humbugs and I sat on a wall outside the shop, sucking on a sweet and writing my postcard as Kip and Ingrid carried on browsing.

SMUGGLER'S COVE

Dear everyone,

    I know you have been here before, but maybe you won't remember that there is a great story about a disappearing smuggler – no one knows how he vanished. I was wondering if you could think of a way for someone to disappear from a locked room with sealed windows without being a ghost? It sounds like one of Doris and Marvin's magic tricks. Anyway, please write back. I really do wish you were here.

    Lots of love

    Poppy xxx

_____
_____
_____
_____
_____

After carefully attaching the stamp I popped the postcard in the shiny red postbox. Finally, we arrived back at the campsite to find everything in chaos. It seemed that somehow *all* of the tents had been knocked down, and while St Smithen's students were good at a lot of things, apparently putting tents back up was not one of them. We found Kip's tent-mate Riley frowning over a couple of tent pegs.

"What happened?" Kip asked.

"Dunno," Riley shrugged, "I just came back and they were all like this, and everyone was in a state because the bathroom block has flooded as well. The plumber's been called out and I think everything's OK now, but we've all got to put our own tents back up and I can only find two of our pegs."

"It's strange that *all* the tents got knocked over." Ingrid wrinkled her nose.

"Yes," I said thoughtfully, "seems unlikely that would happen by accident."

Riley nodded, "That's what Mr Grant and Miss Susan said. They're on the warpath because they reckon one of us lot did it as a prank."

"Why would anyone do that?" Kip asked.

Riley shrugged. A thought suddenly struck

Kip and the colour drained from his face. "No one touched our stuff, did they?" he asked Riley, panicked. "No one stole . . . the sweets?"

Riley clapped a reassuring hand on Kip's shoulder. "It was the first thing I checked, mate. Your haul's intact – down to the last jelly bean."

Kip let out a shuddery sigh of relief. "Thanks, Riley," he said. "You had me worried for a moment."

I rolled my eyes at Ingrid and she nodded in agreement. We made our way to our own tent, which we got straightened out in a jiffy. (I've pitched a few tents in my time at the circus.)

"Who do you think would do something like this?" Ingrid asked.

"I don't know," I said, "but I hope it was just a prank and nothing more. We've already got a mystery to solve!" I couldn't help but think of Henry Redshank's disappearance. Hopefully my circus family would write back with some helpful ideas about the magical disappearing act – and till then at least we had our plan to catch the smugglers in action, that very night!

CHAPTER FIFTEEN

We had arranged to meet near the firepit at midnight, the exact time we'd seen the lights last time. Ingrid and I arrived first, but it wasn't long before we saw the glimmering of Kip's torch approaching. So far there was no sign of any light in the turret or out to sea. Despite the relatively warm evening, when Kip finally appeared he seemed to be wearing everything he owned, including a scarf that was wrapped around his head and tied under his chin, leaving only his face poking out.

"Why are you dressed like that?" I asked, wrinkling my nose. "Aren't you hot?"

"*WELL, I'M NOT ABOUT TO LET A GHOST NEAR ME WITH ITS DEADLY ECTOPLASM, AM*

I?" Kip whispered in the loudest whisper I had ever heard.

"Shhhhh!" I hissed. "No one's getting attacked by deadly ectoplasm, whatever *that* is. We're just investigating. Quietly. But you won't be able to move in all that lot."

Sulkily, Kip undid the scarf and removed his gloves and a couple of jumpers, bundling them in his arms. "I'd better just take these back then," he said.

"Be quick!" I whispered. "You don't want to miss any of the good stuff."

I could hear Kip grumbling over his shoulder as he ran lightly back to his tent, but he was very speedy, and was back (dressed more appropriately) in no time.

"No sign of any lights," Ingrid whispered.

"Let's just give it five more minutes," I said, glancing up at the turret window.

Those five minutes passed verrrrry slowly. (Partly because Kip kept asking if it had been five minutes yet roughly every seven seconds.) Still there was no sign of any light, blue or otherwise. "OK," I said finally. "Let's give up. But I've thought of something else we can do. It's time we had a look around at the beach."

"What? In the middle of the night?" squeaked Kip.

"That's the best possible time!" I exclaimed. "No one will be around, and we can get on with our investigation in secret. How would we explain it if we disappeared in the middle of a surfing lesson? Plus the moon is so bright and the night's so clear we've got a great chance of finding something." Reluctantly Kip and Ingrid acknowledged the merits of my excellent plan. "We've done way scarier things than this," I pointed out helpfully as we made our way to the coastal path by torchlight.

Winding our way down to the beach we passed through the village, which was eerily quiet. I could hear that owl hooting again in a tree nearby, but apart from a couple of street lamps all of the lights seemed to be off. "Well, this is pretty spooky," Kip grumbled, as the three of us stuck close together. He was right, but I knew that all of us were also feeling that familiar thrill of adventure. Ingrid's eyes shone behind her thick glasses, and Kip began to hum his own little theme tune, a sure sign that he was getting into the spirit of things. His eyes lingered on Honeybee's Ice Creamery (he was up to the Ds now, having demolished everything chocolate flavoured that afternoon) as we scurried past, rounding the corner and down the final bit of the path, hitting the sandy beach.

I was right about the moon. It hung over the water like a beautiful shimmering Frisbee, looking bigger and closer than it did when we were at school, and casting everything in a glowing bluish light. The sea was calm, and little waves wriggled across the sand. The tide was far out so the beach felt big and empty.

"What exactly are we looking for?" Kip asked, his voice breaking the quiet.

"Well, there aren't any lights anywhere," Ingrid said. "Which is good . . . or bad? I'm not sure."

"There must be some clue here about Henry's escape," I said, spinning around on the sand. "After all, this is the actual, *real* spot where it happened."

The three of us stood for a moment, letting that thought sink in.

"Do you remember what the guidebook said about the night that Henry Redshank disappeared?" Ingrid said slowly. "Didn't it say that he appeared to vanish into the cliff face?"

We all turned to look at the cliff, looming above us with the castle perched on top.

"You're right," Kip nodded. "It did say that. But

how would you get from down here to up in the castle?"

"There must be a secret tunnel!" I exclaimed, and I knew by the twitching of my nose that I was experiencing what we detectives call "a hunch". "We have to try and find it!"

Kip and Ingrid both nodded in agreement and we began clambering cautiously along the rocks in front of the cliff face, shining our torches and looking for any gaps. It was hard work and it seemed as if we weren't going to have any luck. Suddenly I heard Ingrid's voice calling softly, "Over here!"

Kip and I hustled over to where Ingrid was standing, her torch pointed at a big rock. "What have you found, Ing?" I asked.

"Here," she said, pointing to a tiny gap next to the stone.

"Er, no offence, Ingrid, but I don't think your brain is screwed in properly tonight," Kip said. "No one could fit through there."

"I know that!" Ingrid rolled her eyes. "But look at this." She pointed next to the boulder at a long piece of driftwood that was wedged up against it. Kip and I both looked at her blankly. "I think it might be a lever," she whispered. "You know, to roll this out of the way. It looks like someone has deliberately whittled the bottom to make it thin enough to wedge underneath."

"Really?" Kip asked, but I was nodding.

"I think it could work," I said, picking up the piece of wood and wedging the thin end underneath the stone. I pushed down on the other end with all of my strength and felt it shift a little, but I couldn't get it to move. "I think this one's going to be a team effort," I panted.

Kip and Ingrid clambered alongside me, joining in the effort. The rock began to move, and we all pushed as hard as we possibly could. With a final groan the boulder moved to one side, leaving a gap just big enough for a crouched person to fit through. I shone my torch in the gap and bent over to have a look. "It looks like it opens up inside," I said. "Great job, Ing! I would never have spotted that."

Ingrid smiled, but looked nervously at the gap. "I don't know. I don't like the look of it."

"I'll go first," I said bravely, crouching down a little, and shuffling through. As soon as I was on the other side I shone my torch around and found myself standing inside a large cave. "Come through!" I called. "It's huge!"

Ingrid appeared next, quickly followed by Kip.

"Wow!" Kip said, "this is it, isn't it? It's a real smuggler's cave!"

Ingrid looked back at the gap we had crept through. "It is! You'd have to be pretty strong to open the entrance, but if you managed to push the rock over a bit further the gap would easily be big enough to roll barrels of rum through. Just think" – she shone her torch in an arc around us – "we're standing right inside a piece of history!"

"So this is where Henry disappeared to," I mused, looking around.

"But why didn't he just hide out here until the coast was clear?" Ingrid asked.

"Yeah, why did he go up to the castle?" Kip looked puzzled, and I had to agree it had been a strange plan.

Just then there was a groaning sound from behind us, and the boulder rolled back across the entrance, extinguishing all the light except that of our torches.

A small squeaking noise escaped Kip's lips.

"Well," I gulped, trying to sound cheerful. "Looks like there's only one way out of here." I shone my torch into the dark and forbidding passageway that lay ahead. "Shall we see where this goes?"

CHAPTER SIXTEEN

The ground was sandy, and the walls of the cave were high and cool. At the back of the cave was the mouth of a long, dark tunnel. We began to creep silently towards it when, suddenly, Kip exclaimed, "What's that?"

In the shadows I saw a dark shape against the wall of the cave. Shining the torch on it revealed a black tarpaulin sheet that seemed to be covering something. "This must be the goods that they were bringing ashore last night!" I exclaimed. "That's why the signals were lit!" I knew in my bones that we had stumbled across the smugglers' terrible hoard. What could it be? A pile of stolen jewels? A hoard of careful art forgeries? Priceless antiques stuffed into brandy barrels? With a flourish I twitched the corner of the sheet back, revealing ... a big pile of tin cans all neatly stacked.

"What are these doing here?!" I exclaimed, picking up a can for a closer look and giving it a shake. Much to my dismay it didn't make a tinkling noise to indicate it was full of pristine diamonds. No, the faint sloshing only confirmed what the label had to say ... it was a tin of chicken soup.

"Well, that settles it," Ingrid said. "Someone has definitely been here recently. I don't think those tins of chicken soup are two hundred and fifty years old."

"But why would anyone want to smuggle tins of food and hide them down here?" I puzzled, picking up other cans of baked beans and spaghetti hoops.

"And who has been coming down here in the first place? I doubt chicken soup is popular with the ghostly community, so at least it seems like we are dealing with a real person." Ingrid pushed her glasses up her nose.

Kip nodded wisely. "I think ghosts are only interested in munching on human brains, so this probably doesn't belong to ghost smugglers."

"I think that's zombies," I said. "I'm not sure ghosts eat anything."

"Imagine not being able to eat ANYTHING!" Kip shuddered. "I never want to be a ghost. You'd be drifting around all day seeing people eating all the best food and you couldn't even have a tiny little bite of cake or anything. No wonder ghosts are always supposed to be all sad and angry. . . I get like that when I'm hungry too." He looked thoughtful. "Maybe someone should invent, like, ghost biscuits or something and then nowhere would ever be haunted by mean spirits. They'd all be really friendly and help you with the washing-up—"

"Anyway!" said Ingrid, interrupting before Kip could develop his marketing strategy for GhostBiscuits™. "If there are modern-day smugglers using this cave, they must be connected to the lights we saw the other night. So that means . . . whoever was in the turret room was no ghost."

Ingrid was right, but we were no closer to finding out who that person was.

"Maybe there are more clues further in?" I suggested, illuminating the mouth of the tunnel with my torch once more.

"Only one way to find out," said Ingrid, and Kip swallowed hard. "Let's go!"

As we made our way along in single file, my

excited voice bounced off the narrow walls of the tunnel. "This *must* be the tunnel that Henry used to reach Crumley Castle!"

"Yes, we do seem to be going uphill, and in the right direction." Ingrid's voice came from behind me, and she was right, the tunnel turned steeply up at a sharp angle. We crept further along, until we reached a fork and the tunnel split in two, both paths carrying on further uphill.

"Hmmm," I pursed my lips thoughtfully. "Which way, do you think?"

"Let's go right," Kip piped up, "the tunnel looks wider that way." We turned right and carried along for another minute or two. Kip was right: the tunnel was wider here, and there were some very old-looking wooden beams along the walls and overhead. Finally, after walking for what felt like for ever, we almost bumped smack into a solid brick wall. "Noooooo!" I hissed. I ran my hands over it and felt cool, slightly damp and very unyielding stone. My heart sank. I was so sure we were on to something but the massive wall in front of me was the deadest of dead ends. It was a huge disappointment.

"I guess this is the end," I sighed, turning to

face the others and leaning back against the wall. "Should we—" My sentence was cut short as a brick moved beneath my elbow with a low *click*, and the wall began sliding silently to one side.

I turned and we all watched open-mouthed as the wall moved, revealing a small entrance. "A secret passageway!" Ingrid whispered.

Dim light spilled into the tunnel and we could see we were behind some kind of heavy green tapestry. I was about to shriek with amazement when I realized that I could hear a voice on the other side of it – and not just any voice, but a very familiar one. It was Miss Susan!

We must be behind the tapestry in Agatha's study, I thought, recognizing the colour. But what on earth was Miss Susan doing there at way past midnight? This was hardly normal, teacherly behaviour, plus our whole plan had been based on the idea that all the grown-ups would be tucked up safely in their beds. I swung back to face Kip and Ingrid, my finger on my lips. They both nodded and we all shuffled forward as quietly as possible to listen to the conversation that was taking place.

"I just don't understand why we needed to meet like this, in secret and in the middle of the night,"

Miss Susan was saying in a low voice. "Something is obviously very wrong, Agatha. Why don't you tell me what is going on?"

"I don't know if I can!" Agatha's nervous voice replied, and she sounded high-pitched and tearful. "Oh, Elaine, it's just so terrible – I don't know what to do!" Agatha dissolved into tears here, and there was a pause in which we heard Miss Susan make some murmured, soothing noises. This was followed by some quiet snuffling as Agatha blew her nose.

"Come on, Aggie, you know you can tell me anything," Miss Susan was saying now. "You and I have never had any secrets from one another, remember?" This made my heart skip a beat. If Miss Susan really told Agatha everything, did that mean she had told her about *me*? Did Agatha know that Miss Susan had had a baby, a little girl, and that she had left her at a travelling circus? I held my breath, half desperately hoping that they would start talking about it, and half desperately hoping that they wouldn't. Instead of discussing Miss Susan's dark secret past, however, there was the sound of Agatha blowing her nose again.

"You're right," she murmured finally, "there's something I need to show you," and there was the scraping sound of her chair being pulled back. We pressed ourselves tight against the wall, in case she came too close to our hiding place. Instead she seemed to be opening a drawer and rifling through some papers – she must be going through her desk, I realized. "Here," she said, her footsteps crossing the room again. There was another pause and then Miss Susan let out a horrified gasp.

"Agatha! Is this real?"

"Yes, I'm afraid so," said Agatha heavily, and there came the sound of more tears spilling over. "It's – well, you can see for yourself – it's a ransom note. Darling Jenny's been kidnapped!"

CHAPTER SEVENTEEN

The Booths' daughter had been kidnapped! Kip, Ingrid and I had to stifle gasps of our own. I strained to hear the rest of Agatha and Miss Susan's conversation.

"I – I can't believe it!" Miss Susan's voice was frightened. It was not a tone I had heard her use before, and it made my stomach flutter nervously. She began reading from the note, her voice hushed. "I have your daughter. No harm will come to her unless you call the police…" There was a stunned silence, and then Miss Susan spoke again. "When did you realize she was missing?"

"Just before you arrived," Agatha's voice wobbled. "We have no idea how they got to her."

"Why haven't you called the police?" Miss Susan asked.

"You've read the note!" exclaimed Agatha. "They said if we do they'll hurt Jenny! They said that they're watching us! How can we risk it?!" She started crying again. "I wanted to anyway, but Bernard doesn't think we should take the chance. He's beside himself with worry."

"I'm sure you both are," Miss Susan said, and she sounded stunned. "I can't believe you've been keeping this a secret. Are you going to pay the ransom?"

Agatha whimpered. "If only we could. But we don't have that sort of money . . . nowhere near."

"But the inheritance. . ." Miss Susan murmured. "Surely that would cover it?"

"There *is* no inheritance!" Agatha sobbed. "After all the bills were paid, there was so little left over. Of course Bernard inherited the castle, but the place is falling down around us and the cost of running it is astronomical. Everyone seems to think that we've inherited a fortune, and that we're using our mountain of cash to do the place up, but the truth is we've never been worse off!"

"Do you have any idea who is behind the kidnapping?" Miss Susan asked.

"None at all." Agatha sighed. "We can't even work out how they did it. We all saw Jenny go to bed that evening, but in the morning she had just gone. *Vanished*."

"Someone must have gone into her room," Miss Susan suggested.

"Impossible!" Agatha cried, then lowering her voice, she continued, "Jenny's room was locked ... *from the inside*. The key was still in the door! We didn't know anything had happened until we got the note. You know teenagers, sometimes they don't leave their rooms for days. Bernard had to break the lock in the end, and she was ... *gone*." Agatha was sobbing quietly again now. "To be honest, I'm starting to hate this place." She sniffled. "We feel so unwelcome! I'm beginning to believe all this talk about dark forces being at work here. Things keep going wrong. You saw what happened at the campsite today with all the tents falling down and the pipes in the bathrooms breaking. That's only the latest problem; it's been one disaster after another. And we can't shake off Stanley Goodwill because he's lived here for years, and Fuddling is so cold towards us. And now my darling Jenny. It's all just too much!"

"I had no idea you were under so much pressure," Miss Susan said. "You've done all the work on the campsite, it looks so good. . ."

"But the campsite is part of the problem," said Agatha, and there was the gentle *thud* of her sitting back heavily in her chair. "We wanted to keep the castle going – we couldn't bear the thought of losing it, so we decided to turn it into a business. We knew people would want to come and stay here, and the grounds are such a beautiful place to camp. Of course, we had to borrow an awful lot of money from the bank, and they're breathing down our necks to make sure we repay them. We had so many problems with all the building work, you wouldn't believe it. Equipment went missing, something seemed to have chewed through all our new wiring, then one of the builders broke his leg when a ladder wasn't secured properly. It was problem after problem, and every accident meant paying out more money. We desperately need the camping business to succeed, but we have absolutely no money to spare . . . let alone enough to pay off these kidnappers. What will we do? Oh, my poor, poor Jenny. . ." She trailed off hopelessly.

"Who else knows about this?" Miss Susan asked.

"No one," Agatha whispered. "Only Bernard and I. And now you."

And the three of us, I added silently, glancing at Kip and Ingrid, whose faces mirrored the shock that I was feeling.

"You know your secret is safe with me," Miss Susan said heavily, "and we *will* find a solution. I promise. Nothing will happen to Jenny. You'll see."

"Thank you," snuffled Agatha. "I'm glad I told you. It's been so hard keeping it a secret. . . I thought I was going to go mad!"

Their voices were getting further away now as they walked towards the door, and clicked off the light.

"Try and get some sleep," Miss Susan said soothingly, her voice just reaching my ears in the darkness. "We'll talk about it again tomorrow. And there might be something I can do to help; I know a very good detective." For one dazzling moment I thought she was talking about me, but my bubble was quickly burst when Miss Susan continued. "His name is Inspector Hartley and I think he may be able to help us." With this they shut the door behind them and were gone.

Kip, Ingrid and I stood frozen for a couple more minutes in total darkness, listening carefully to make sure the coast was clear before tumbling through the opening and into the study. The secret door slid shut behind us with a gentle *thud*. I felt around and found a light switch on the wall, snapping the lights back on. The three of us stood blinking at one another in silence. You would never have known the door was there at all. It looked just like a normal wall.

"Woah," Kip said finally, and Ingrid and I both nodded very dazed nods.

"I can't believe that just happened," I said, my voice coming out a bit squeaky.

"I know." Ingrid sounded squeaky too. "A secret tunnel *and* a kidnapping. This has been a busy night." She nodded at the door behind us. "Well we know one thing. This must have been how Henry Redshank entered the castle. He disappeared from that spot in the cliff face. . ."

"But if that were true he'd have had to walk right past Moira Booth because she was sitting in here, reading," I pondered. Something about this just didn't add up.

"And the cook said she saw him in the hallway *before* he ran into the library," Ingrid said.

"Perhaps he went the other way in the tunnel?" Kip suggested. "We don't know where that comes out yet."

"That's true," Ingrid agreed, "and then he must have run into the library and escaped back down this tunnel, after Moira fainted."

"Can you open it from this side, do you reckon?" I asked, pressing against every single stone on the wall where the door had been, looking for the tiniest crack or some kind of switch. There was nothing. We searched the rest of the room, pushing every stone, trying every way we could think of, but the door didn't budge.

"Maybe it only opens from the inside?" Kip shrugged.

It certainly looked like Kip was right. "And there I was thinking we had solved Henry Redshank's mysterious disappearance from the locked library!" I exclaimed. "But if you can't get out of this room using the tunnel, it wouldn't have been much help to him, would it? And why would he come up from the beach to the castle just to go back down to the beach again? It doesn't make any sense."

"There is one thing," I said thoughtfully, a moment later. "Do you think the secret tunnel could be connected to Jenny's disappearance?"

"But she went missing from her room, not the study," said Ingrid.

"But the tunnel did go in another direction," Kip pointed out eagerly. "We went right – what if the left one goes to Jenny's room? Perhaps Henry Redshank got into the castle that way?"

"You're right," I breathed. "Maybe if we find out where the other tunnel goes we can help to get her back."

Kip and Ingrid both nodded. "Yes," said Ingrid. "Let's hope so. Poor Agatha! She sounded so scared. And poor Jenny! Imagine being taken away from your parents like that."

Ingrid's words hung in the air and for a second it felt like a knife had twisted in my stomach, but I reminded myself firmly not to be so dramatic. Mine and Jenny's situations were totally different and, instead of focusing on myself, my number one priority had to be helping to rescue Jenny – that's exactly what Dougie Valentine would do.

"Perhaps we should just peek at the ransom note?" I suggested after a moment. "There might be a clue there that only we can spot." I was already moving over to the desk as if drawn there by an invisible magnet. Pulling the drawer slowly open, I leafed through some boring-looking documents before pulling out a sheet of crumpled paper. It was covered in a message made from letters cut from newspapers and magazines.

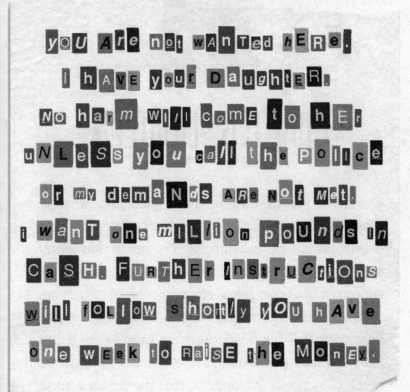

YOU ARe not wANTed hERe.
I hAVE your DaughtER.
No harm wIll COmE to hEr
uNLeSs you call the POlIce
or my demaNds ARe Not met.
i waNT one mILLIOn poUNds In
CaSH. FuRThEr InstruCtiOns
wIll fOllow shoRtly. yOu hAVe
one WEek to RaiSE the MONey.

"Woah," Kip said again.

That pretty much summed it up.

CHAPTER EIGHTEEN

Of course, we were in a bit of a quandary when it came to offering our help in Jenny's disappearance. *Technically* we weren't supposed to know that Jenny was missing at all, and we also weren't *technically* supposed to have been creeping out of our tents in the middle of the night to go hunting for ghost smugglers ... but here we were, and with Jenny in potentially grave danger there didn't seem to be much of a choice. We decided that the next morning I would have a quiet word with Miss Susan and tell her about the secret tunnels that we thought must have played a part in the kidnapping.

At least, that was the plan. But the next morning Miss Susan was nowhere to be seen. I asked Mr

Grant if he knew where she was and he shook his head. "Miss Susan had something to take care of," he said lightly and I knew straight away that she hadn't told him about Jenny's kidnapping – he looked far too cheerful. "Now hurry up, Poppy!" he exclaimed. "You've got a surfing lesson to get ready for."

And so, the three of us found ourselves back down in Smuggler's Cove, squeezed into our wetsuits, having a surfing lesson with the dreamy Jack Jenkins. At least Annabelle and her friends seemed to find Jack pretty dreamy – they kept asking him to come and show them again how to jump up on their surfboards, which were laid out in a line on the sand between rows of orange markers. Thanks to my gymnastics training I was finding all the leaping about quite easy, but Kip and Ingrid were concentrating deeply. We all had turns running into the sea with our boards and riding in from shallower waters, then we sat in the sand and watched Mr Grant and Jack show off their surfing skills. Everyone cheered as they glided in and leapt about on top of foam-capped waves. I tried to enjoy myself, but my brain was very full, and my eyes kept drifting over to the big rock that hid the entrance cave and the tunnels up to the castle. I could just about make it out, but only because I knew where it was – to a casual observer it would look like any other rock. Had the tunnel really played a part in Jenny's kidnapping? We had only followed one part of the tunnel, after all, and I was itching to find out where the other part went. I felt certain it was an important piece of the puzzle ... one that may well help us to solve *both* our mysteries.

I was so deep in thought that I didn't notice the others were moving back to the water to have another go on their surfboards. I was shaken out of my musings by the arrival of Jack Jenkins, who appeared at my side brushing water out of his very blue eyes. "Poppy, isn't it? You looked like a natural out there earlier!" he said warmly. "Have you surfed before?" He smiled his easy smile, and I could feel the corners of my mouth tugging up in response. OK, I thought grudgingly, maybe I could see some of the appeal.

I shook my head in answer to his question. "No. But . . . but it is really fun," I said lamely.

"Best feeling in the world!" he replied.

Mr Grant appeared then, running out of the water towards us with his surfboard tucked under his arm.

"You were really good, sir!" I exclaimed.

"Thank you, Poppy," Mr Grant said. "Not as good as this young man though!" He slapped Jack on the shoulder.

"Thanks," Jack replied, with a pleased smile spreading across his face, like a dimmer switch being turned up on full beam. "I want to do it professionally, you know. I'm saving up to open my own surf school on some amazing tropical island. Surf all day... Heaven!"

"Sounds good to me," Mr Grant agreed. "Maybe we could open a surf school at Saint Smithen's?" He smiled at me.

"Except we're nowhere near the sea," I pointed out.

"Ah yes," Mr Grant replied. "There is that little problem. I don't suppose the school pond will do?"

"Not a lot of waves in the pond," I said glumly, because it really would be a lot of fun to learn how to surf like Mr Grant and Jack did.

Mr Grant laughed. "I'd better round up the troops," he said to Jack. "Poppy, will you help Jack to tidy the equipment?"

I nodded as Mr Grant started back towards the group, already reaching for his trusty silver whistle.

I went with Jack to help retrieve the orange markers from the sand.

"Hey, weren't you the kid asking about the smugglers?" he asked suddenly.

"Yep," I answered. It seemed like a long time since I had asked Jack about the Redshank brothers, and an awful lot had happened in that time.

"Why so interested?" Jack asked. "Are you some sort of history buff?"

"No, not really," I said. "I just read about it in the guidebook and it seemed like a good story."

"Oh right," Jack said, scratching his cheek. There was another pause. "Are you enjoying your stay up at the castle?" he asked.

"It's a pretty amazing place." I grinned. "Imagine living somewhere like that!"

"Yeah," Jack nodded, shielding his eyes with his hand and looking up the hill to the castle. "It would really be something."

"Hey, do you know Jenny Booth?" I asked suddenly, deciding that perhaps I should be asking a few questions of my own while I had the opportunity.

Jack froze, his hand still next to his face. "Jenny Booth?" His voice sounded a bit strange and distant.

"Er, yes," I said. "She lives up at the castle. I thought you two were sort of the same age so..."

"Yeah, of course I know Jenny," Jack said in a voice that was a bit too big and too loud, like a piece of clothing that didn't quite fit right. "I do some gardening and odd jobs up at the castle so I've seen her around. Why do you want to know?"

"Oh, er, s-sorry," I stuttered. "We were just talking about living in the castle and she does, so I was just ... interested."

Why was he behaving so strangely? I wondered.

"Seems like you're interested in a lot of things," Jack said lightly.

"Ohhhh Jaaaaack!" Annabelle trilled from behind us. "We need your help." I could practically feel the gust of wind created by her batting eyelashes from here, but for once I was glad for Annabelle's interference.

"Curious," I muttered under my breath as Jack walked away. It seemed to me like Crumley was just bursting with mysteries and people keeping secrets.

I didn't have time to dwell on this, however, because just then a cry tore through the air.

I swivelled my head to the side, alert and ready for action. Someone had obviously met with a horrific accident and I was ready to spring to their aid. Instead I saw Kip with both fists raised in the air. "Yahoooooooooooooo!" he yelled. "It's Mrs Crockton!" He pointed, and there she was, coming down the path and carrying an enormous hamper.

"Lunchtime!" yelled Mr Grant, running over the sand to help Mrs Crockton with her basket.

"I know what the sea air does to you," Mrs Crockton said with a smile, "so I've got pasties, and jam splits for pudding." There was an anxious pause. "I didn't have time to make them myself, I'm afraid," she said, sighing. "They're from the bakery." Hopefully she didn't notice the enormous collective sigh of relief.

"What a feast!" I said, munching on my warm pasty, my hair a wet and salty tangle and my toes burrowing into the sand. "I don't think I've ever been so hungry!"

"I *know*!" exclaimed Kip. "I thought I was going to have to chew off my own arm. Do you think we're only allowed one pasty each, or do you reckon Mrs Crockton got extra?"

"Maybe you should go and ask," I said with a giggle. "You're very quiet, Ing," I said, after Kip had left on a pasty quest of great importance.

"Sorry," Ingrid said, her eyes losing their dreamy look and coming in to focus on my face. "It's just. . . I can't stop thinking about poor Jenny Booth. Do you think the tunnels are connected to her kidnapping?"

"I don't know," I admitted. "What do you think we should do?"

"I think we need to speak to Miss Susan," she said. "Everyone seems to have something to hide."

"Speaking of which. . ." I filled her in on my strange conversation with Jack. "It might be nothing," I said in conclusion. "But he seemed shifty to me. I think it's time to bring in Miss Susan."

"Well, now's our chance," Ingrid said slowly. "Because here she comes."

CHAPTER NINETEEN

I took a deep breath and made my way over to Miss Susan who was talking quietly with Mr Grant. It went against all my detective instincts to share our findings with Miss Susan at this early stage, and then there was still the little, unresolved matter of her being my mother and all, but a girl was missing and I knew that finding her was the most important thing.

"Why are you hovering, Poppy?" Miss Susan said, slightly irritably.

"Oh!" I exclaimed, thrown by her stern tone. "Er, sorry, miss," I said, "but I – I just need to, er..."

"Yes?" Miss Susan asked, her eyebrows raised.

"I need to talk to you about something," I managed to squeak out. My voice sounded like a grumpy toddler's.

Miss Susan's face seemed to soften a bit. "Come on then," she said with a sigh, "let's go and have a cup of tea up at the castle. But first" – her eyes ran over my bedraggled form – "you had better go and clean up a bit. I will meet you in the entrance hall in ten minutes."

I scampered up to the campsite, washed and changed into a pair of purple shorts and an orange T-shirt with a speed that would have impressed a cheetah at the top of his game. Nine and a half minutes later I was waiting for Miss Susan in the echoey entrance hall. Fuddling materialized silently through one of the doors and looked at me over the top of his glasses as if I was a sticky child waiting to mess up all of the furniture.

"Can I help you?" he said, in a voice that made it sound like he didn't want to help me very much with anything – except leaving.

"I'm waiting for Miss Susan," I said primly. "I'm meeting her here."

"Hmph," said Fuddling, evidently unimpressed by this response.

"So . . . I hear you've worked here for a long time?" I said, trying to make small talk.

"I suppose some people might call forty years a long time." He sniffed.

"Wow," I said blankly, casting around for something to say. "Forty years *is* a long time, isn't it? Not that it's *that* long, I mean. Not that you're old." I laughed awkwardly and my voice was getting a bit squeaky. "Because you're not, obviously. . ." I trailed off. "You're practically young – very, erm, spry. . ."

"Hmph," Fuddling said again. Apparently he agreed that my small talk attempts weren't going well. I was relieved when Stanley Goodwill wandered through, his nose in a book and his thinning hair sticking out in all directions. Fuddling melted away.

"Ah, hello!" Stanley said when he spotted me (or I should say, after he walked into me). "How'd you get on with that book?"

"Oh, it was brilliant! Thank you, Mr Goodwill," I said with a winning smile. "So interesting! And so exciting to read a real account of the smuggler's disappearance."

"Not at all, not at all! Delighted!" He shook my

hand. "It's always a pleasure to share some of the history of this place."

"It really is an amazing building," I agreed.

"Oh, it's so much more than that." Stanley's eyes shone. "It's a legacy you know, one that it's our sacred duty to protect. We must take care of it, preserve it and not let the contraptions of modern life corrupt it. The place shouldn't be treated like some sort of hotel." He said the word like it was something truly distasteful, and suddenly his face looked as though he had bitten down on a sour lemon. Just then a group of noisy students tore through the hallway, one of them bumping against Stanley on his way past. Stanley glared.

"Don't you like the campsite?" I asked carefully.

The sour-lemon look disappeared, and was replaced by Stanley's watery smile. "Oh no, dear," he said. "I think it's a fine idea and I'm sure it will be a big success. *Dear* Agatha and Bernard have worked so hard on it. Now, where have I put my glasses?" He started patting his pockets.

"They're round your neck," I said helpfully, pointing to them on their little cord.

Stanley looked surprised. "Oh, lovely," he said. "Best be getting back to work." He tapped the cover of his book which looked quite dull and like it contained absolutely no pictures at all. Just then Miss Susan arrived and Stanley scuttled off.

"Hello, Poppy. I thought we would go up to my room for a bit of privacy." Miss Susan's voice was almost friendly. She led the way up two flights of stairs and down a corridor on the left. Her room was nice and airy with a view of the sea from a big window. The walls were papered in pale green paper dotted with little flowers and the floorboards were bare. It was a large room but it didn't have much furniture in it, only a bed, a wardrobe and a small table with two white wicker chairs pulled up by the window. Miss Susan gestured for me to have a seat in one of these just as there was a knock on the door. It was Mrs Crockton carrying a tray of gently steaming tea.

"Ah, thank you!" Miss Susan said, lifting the tray out of her hands. "I'll bring it down when we're finished."

"No bother, duck," Mrs Crockton said, winking at me over Miss Susan's shoulder and bustling back down the corridor.

Miss Susan settled opposite me and poured two mugs of tea. "Now, Poppy," she said, leaning back and blowing on her drink, "what did you need to talk to me about?"

"Yes," I said. "Right. Well, it's actually a bit awkward. And a bit . . . complicated. . ."

"I see," she said expectantly. "Go on."

"OK," I began, taking a deep breath and starting at the beginning, just as I had practised in my head. "Well, the thing is that before we came here I was reading in this book, about these smugglers called the Redshank brothers—"

"Smugglers?" Miss Susan said coldly, and I saw a frown beginning.

"Yes, they were from Crumley and one of them, called Henry, disappeared from the castle—"

Miss Susan put her mug down with a *thud* and held up her hand. "*This* is what you wanted to talk to me about?" she exclaimed. "Smugglers?"

"Yes, but—" I tried to explain, but Miss Susan was squeezing the bridge of her nose between her thumb and forefinger.

"Honestly, Poppy!" she snapped, "I thought this was something imporrrrtant! I'm very busy, you know, and there's a lot going on – a lot of *serious* things."

"I know!" I exclaimed. "That's why I'm trying

to tell you. It all started with the smugglers, it was a mystery you see, but then we realized..." I was interrupted again by Miss Susan's humourless laugh.

"A mystery? Oh, showing off and chasing after trouble again, Poppy? When will you learn?" She got to her feet. "I'm sorry, but I just can't think about this at the moment. Frankly, I have a terrible headache and a lot on my mind, and I don't have time for you and your silliness."

And suddenly I had had enough. Something big and angry was welling up from deep inside me and this time there was no way to stuff it back down. I leapt to my feet.

"Oh no, you'd never have time for ME, would you?" I shouted right at her, and her anger was replaced with a look of astonishment.

"What ... what is that supposed to mean?" she said, her hand moving to her throat.

"I think you *know* what that's supposed to mean!" I yelled then, because yelling felt really, *really* good.

"I absolutely do not," said Miss Susan, two pink spots appearing on her cheeks. "And I won't be spoken to like this, Poppy. You're out of line. I'm your teacher."

"I know who you are," I muttered dangerously,

and a silence as sharp as peanut brittle filled the room.

Then the pink spots on Miss Susan's cheeks got darker, or the rest of her face got paler – or maybe a combination of the two.

"I think you are overexcited, Poppy," Miss Susan said shakily. "You had better go and calm down."

But it was too late. My anger was bubbling over like a saucepan full of rage porridge.

"I am not overexcited," I shouted. "I am telling you that I know your secret!"

Miss Susan gasped and sank back into the chair, her head in her hands. "Poppy. . ." she said sadly, but I didn't let her say anything else.

"I know the truth." I finally said the words out loud. "I know that you're my mother."

CHAPTER TWENTY

I was shaking now, and the room was silent again, but it was a different kind of silence. Miss Susan got to her feet.

"Poppy," she began, and I steeled myself for what came next, waiting for her to tell me why she had left me at the circus, why she had kept me a secret, why she hadn't told me herself.

Instead she said, "I'm sorry, Poppy. I know you think... I mean, I have to tell you..." She trailed off hopelessly here before taking a deep breath. "I am *not* your mother," she said finally, and her voice sounded cold and distant.

It felt as if all of the air had been bashed right out of me. "W-w-what?" I asked, in a daze.

"I said: I am not your mother," Miss Susan repeated.

I felt tears welling up inside me, threatening to burst out at any moment. "You're . . . you're lying. I know you are!" I gasped.

Miss Susan was still pale, and her mouth was set in a thin, straight line. "I'm not lying, Poppy, it's the truth. I'm not the person you're looking for." Her voice was flat and empty.

I stared at her. She *must* be lying. The necklace – and the photograph. . .

The truth was, she hadn't wanted me then, and she didn't want me now. The room began to spin, and with my knees trembling beneath me I ran out of the door as fast as I could.

"No, Poppy. Wait! We need to talk!" Miss Susan called after me, but I just kept on going. I couldn't stand to be near her for a single moment longer. I ran along the corridor, and down the stairs, through the entrance hall, and the gardens, around the winding coastal path, past the village and out on to the empty beach. I ran and ran without stopping until my lungs felt like they were on fire, and when I reached the water I shouted out into the sea in a voice as big as I had left. Then I sat down on the sand and cried.

I don't know how long I sat there, but eventually I stood up and dusted myself off. I felt determination coursing through me like cherry cola through a twisty straw. If Miss Susan wanted to pretend she wasn't my mother then that was just fine by me. I hadn't needed her for the last twelve years and I wasn't about to start needing her now.

On top of the feelings of sadness and hurt there was another feeling, an angry feeling. Before we had even had our fight Miss Susan had refused to listen to me . . . even when I was trying to help solve a kidnapping. What had she said? *Showing off and chasing after trouble again.* I stuck my chin out and pulled my shoulders down. Well, we'd just see about that. We would just have to save Jenny ourselves, and then when Miss Susan finally realized just how completely brilliant I was, THEN I would tell her exactly what I thought of her. I spun on my heel and stomped back up towards the castle. I needed to find Kip and Ingrid. We had work to do.

"What do you mean you didn't tell her?" Ingrid asked when I had found them waiting for me in the castle gardens. She frowned over her glasses at me.

"I mean, she wouldn't listen," I said. "I tried to

tell her, but she just said I was showing off and chasing mysteries again, and she was too busy and she didn't have time for me." I left out the rest of the conversation for obvious reasons. I could already feel hot tears prickling behind my eyelids and I told myself sternly that I could *not* cry in front of Kip and Ingrid. Then they'd definitely want to know what was going on.

"Oh dear," Ingrid said glumly. "Well, I think we should try and talk to her again and really make her listen."

"I told you," I snapped. "She's not interested in helping. We're better off without her."

Ingrid looked surprised by my outburst. "I only meant—" she began.

"I know what you meant," I interrupted, and suddenly my voice came out sounding small. "But you weren't there. She won't listen. I tried but. . ." I trailed off miserably.

There was silence then. Kip and Ingrid exchanged a look.

"Are you all right, Poppy?" Kip piped up cautiously. "You seem a bit . . . well, not yourself."

"I'm fine," I said, and I tried to inject a bit more cheerfulness into my voice, "but if Miss Susan isn't going to take us seriously, we had better solve the whole thing ourselves. It's the only way to help Jenny and her parents. We just have to find the kidnapper and rescue Jenny. Easy."

"Oh yeah. *Easy*," Kip said, but he smiled and nudged me with his elbow.

"OK," said Ingrid, taking a deep breath. "Where do we start?"

"Well I think the first thing is to check out the tunnel and the path we didn't take last night. It might lead to Jenny's room." The others nodded. "We've got a bit of free time before dinner – let's go now!" I added.

They both agreed, and we darted out in the direction of the path – almost bashing into Jack Jenkins who was coming up to the castle, a toolbox in his hand.

"Careful!" he said lightly. "Where are you lot off to?"

"Um – nowhere!" I said, flashing him a ginormous smile. "What are you doing here?"

He grinned. "I'm here to fix a lamp." He lifted the toolbox and gave it a little shake. "Are you lot sneaking off to get ice cream?" he whispered.

"Yes! Busted!" I whispered back, raising a finger

to my lips. "Don't tell! We're not supposed to leave the grounds unsupervised."

"Your secret's safe with me," he said, moving towards the castle. "Try the sticky toffee cheesecake flavour. It'll blow your mind."

We escaped down towards the village. Kip was uncharacteristically silent, his bottom lip stuck out a little. "Is something wrong?" I asked him.

"It's what Jack said," he answered despondently.

"I don't think he'll tell on us, don't worry," I said, trying to be reassuring.

"Not that," he wailed. "It's the ice cream! I'll never make it to S in my alphabetized mission at this rate, and sticky toffee cheesecake flavour sounds AMAZING."

"Fine," I said. "One *quick* ice cream stop and *then* we solve the mystery." After all, I reasoned, it was no good trying to fight crime on an empty stomach.

Kip beamed. Moments later we emerged from Honeybee's clutching waffle cones: sticky toffee cheesecake for me and Ingrid, ginger nut and honeycomb for Kip. "Gahhhhhh!" I mumbled through a delicious mouthful. "This is amazing! Kip, you should definitely have had one!"

"No way!" Kip exclaimed. "If you're not going to take it seriously and stick to the system then you don't DESERVE THE ICE CREAM. It's the only way to be truly scientific about it. Plus," he added, stuffing his face, "this is pretty good too." He pulled out a little card from his pocket.

"What's that?" I asked.

"I started keeping a score card with tasting notes, just to be thorough," he said, and he slurped on his ice cream thoughtfully. "I'm giving this one four out of five for flavour and five out of five for mouth feel." He handed me his ice cream briefly while he made a note.

"Mouth feel?" I whispered to Ingrid, and she shrugged.

We managed to demolish our cones by the time we reached the entrance to the cave, and I think we were all feeling revived by the health-giving benefits of delicious ice cream. We found the entrance easily enough and this time we knew exactly how to open it. Rolling the rock out of the way we pulled out our trusty torches once more and entered the cave. The stack of tins was still there, and nothing else had been disturbed. There was a familiar groaning sound, and the entrance to the cave sealed behind us. Now the space we were standing in was blacker than black and our torches cut tremulous golden shapes in the darkness.

"Still spooky." Kip's voice bounced off the walls, echoing back to us over and over again like the cries of an unhappy ghost.

"Er, yep," I whispered dryly. "Let's not make it any worse, eh!"

Kip placed the torch beneath his chin and pulled the most gruesome face he could manage.

Ingrid and I giggled weakly. It would be funnier when we were back out in the sunlight.

Without another word the three of us began making our way up the tunnel until we came to the fork where we had turned right the day before.

"Here goes nothing!" I said, taking the left turn. The tunnel got pretty narrow this way, and the three of us walked in single file, our torches carving an arc of light on the ground in front of us. Then, just as we had before, we reached what appeared to be a dead end – only this time we knew better. "Now, where do you think the secret switch will be?" I muttered, pressing on the different bricks. Finally, one near the bottom moved in slightly, and the wall began to slide silently to the left, revealing a room beyond.

There was no tapestry this time and as we moved forward the door slid closed behind us. Fortunately for us the room appeared to be empty. Unfortunately, it definitely *wasn't* Jenny's bedroom.

"Where are we?" Kip hissed.

"I have no idea," I whispered. "But I don't like it."

Just then, Kip gasped. "Arghhhh!" he cried, his voice shrill. "Is that . . . a bear?"

CHAPTER TWENTY-ONE

Kip was right – it was a bear. It stood towering over us in the corner to our left, its mouth open in a ferocious snarl and its claws extended – it was terrifying. Fortunately it was also dead and stuffed. There were many other stuffed animal heads lining one of the long walls. Foxes, badgers and deer with big antlers all stared down at us with glassy, vacant eyes.

"Well, this place isn't creepy at all," I muttered sarcastically, then I jumped as a large grandfather clock began to chime four o'clock. (Although maybe chime is the wrong word, it was actually more like a dusty wheeze.)

"But, where *are* we?" Kip asked again. "This can't be Jenny's room."

"Doesn't look like a typical seventeen-year-old's room to me," I said, looking around. "Unless Jenny's really into dead stuff."

The room was high-ceilinged and long, with large windows that were covered in heavy red velvet drapes blocking out most of the sunshine. What little light filtered through had a faintly red glow which only added to the room's creepy feel. There was some battered but comfortable-looking furniture – a couple of old sofas and armchairs covered in a faded floral pattern drawn near a huge ornate fireplace, and a table on which bottles of alcohol stood next to some glasses. There was also another, smaller table with an old-fashioned telephone next to the sofa, and to the right of us a pile of large, old chests with big iron padlocks. The room was finished off with a number of moth-eaten animal-skin rugs (heads still very much attached).

Ingrid had pulled a sheet of paper from her pocket and was staring at it intently. It was the map that Mr Grant had given us of the castle.

"Given the direction we came in, and the furniture, I think this must be the drawing room," she said, pointing to the map. "The grown-ups use it, but it's off limits to us."

"What a shame." I shivered, trying to avoid all the different animal eyes that were staring right at me.

"Mmm," Ingrid nodded. "It's not very ... homely."

Kip grunted. "Well, that's a bit of an understatement," he said, still nervously eyeing up the bear as though he expected it to attack at any moment.

"So this is the drawing room," I agreed, "but if there's no entrance into Jenny's room, that means that we must have been wrong about the kidnapper using the tunnels..." I trailed off, deep in thought. After all this, were the tunnels and the kidnapping unrelated? My brain couldn't quite work out how everything fitted together – it seemed like there were so many different puzzle pieces to this mystery, and I wasn't even sure that the puzzle pieces were all from the same puzzle at all.

"Does this mean we are still dealing with ghost smugglers as WELL as kidnappers?" Kip didn't sound pleased.

"And speaking of smugglers," I piped up, "do you think THIS is where Henry Redshank came out when he escaped up to the castle?"

Ingrid was looking at the map doubtfully. "I don't think it can be," she said. "Not if the cook ran into him where she said she did in the hallway, he'd have had to be behind her. He *must* have come through the library."

"But how could he if Moira was in there?" Kip said. "Did he sneak past her?"

Before I could answer the three of us froze, as we heard the sound of two pairs of footsteps coming towards the drawing room. How were we going to explain what we were doing here? We all dived for a hiding place. Ingrid and I rather sensibly threw ourselves behind the two large chests to our right. These were big enough to offer good coverage, and I felt like we were pretty well hidden. Kip on the other hand decided for some reason to hide behind the stuffed bear. This was sort of OK because the bear was very big, and Kip was very small (please don't tell him I said that), but it also meant that Kip had to press right up against it, clinging to one enormous leg. He did not look happy about the situation.

The footsteps grew louder, and we heard two different voices.

"Thank you for your help, Jack," the first one said, and it was the low, beefy voice of Horatio Muggins.

"No problem," Jack Jenkins replied. "Just a little issue with the wiring." He must be talking about the lamp he had come up to fix.

"Can I get you a drink?" Horatio asked.

"Let me," Jack replied. "What will you have?"

"Whisky," Horatio said, falling back into one of the sofas with a groan.

More footsteps approached, and I heard a voice that made my blood run cold. "Has anyone seen Agatha?" Miss Susan asked, sounding agitated. I felt a wave of muddled-up feelings wash over me, and had to concentrate very hard on keeping my breathing as quiet as possible.

"Nope," Horatio Muggins replied, taking a swig from his glass. "Get the lady a drink, Jack."

"Sure. What would you like?" Jack asked politely.

"She likes that horrible sweet sherry," Horatio answered with a shudder. "Nasty stuff. No one else will touch it."

"No, thank you," Miss Susan interrupted. "I don't want anything. It's a bit early," she added pointedly.

"Thought you were on your holidays," Horatio said, laughing into his glass.

"I really must find Agatha," Miss Susan huffed, and she turned and left the room.

"Don't know what her problem is," Horatio said after Miss Susan was gone. "Sounds like she could do with a drink."

Jack Jenkins laughed. "Well, I'd better be off too," he said cheerfully. "Let me know if you need anything else doing."

"I will," said Horatio, "thanks for sorting that out. This whole place is a shambles. It all needs some serious work."

"Yeah," Jack agreed, "I guess the Booths will be doing the place up soon with all their inheritance money."

Horatio chuckled at that. "We'll see," he said.

Jack Jenkins left then, and it was just the four of us. I glanced over at Kip who was still well hidden behind the stuffed bear. Ingrid and I were wedged in pretty tight, and my legs were beginning to ache thanks to the awkward position we were squished in. I desperately hoped that Horatio Muggins wouldn't be hanging around for much longer. Unfortunately, I heard the sound of the phone being picked up and the old-fashioned dial spinning around as Horatio dialled a long phone number. After a couple of seconds someone obviously picked up on the other end.

"It's me," Muggins said in a low voice. "Yes, I can talk." There was a pause then as whoever he was speaking to said something. "No, no, no," Muggins said, a bit louder now. "That's not necessary, I have everything under control. You just let me do things my way." There was another pause. "Oh, don't worry about that," he said with an ominous chuckle, as he took another swig from his glass. "They'll pay up. I'll see to that. They'll pay up in full."

CHAPTER TWENTY-TWO

I had to stifle a gasp then, and I saw Kip's head snap back in surprise. Unfortunately, the movement made the bear he was hiding behind tip ever-so-slightly forward and then back into place again. To my ears the tiny *thud* that accompanied this sounded like a massive firework going off, leaving a flashing display behind reading KID DETECTIVES ARE HERE. I held my breath as Muggins paused in his conversation.

"Hello?" he called. "Is someone there?" There was a terrible silence that seemed to go on for ever. I felt my heart clattering away like a noisy typewriter, and I expected to see a threatening shadow looming over us at any moment. Instead, Horatio Muggins returned to his conversation. "Sorry," he said. "Thought I heard something. Anyway, I'm not going anywhere. You just arrange things your end and let me worry about things here. I'll take care of everything. They've got a deadline, and they know the rules, so they'll have to accept our terms... they don't have a choice. No one's been hurt – yet – but they've got to take this seriously." He hung up the phone, and put his empty glass back on the table before leaving the room.

We were alone again. The three of us remained frozen for a while, not wanting to emerge from our hiding places if we were about to find ourselves face-to-face with a dastardly kidnapper. Finally, I poked my head around the side of the trunk. "The coast is clear!" I hissed, unbending myself from the squashed pretzel I had become. Kip and Ingrid followed suit, with Kip pulling away from the giant bear and shaking himself all over.

"That thing smells sooooo bad!" he howled, still wriggling as if he could shake the smell away.

"Phew!" Ingrid exclaimed, pinching her nose, "and now so do you!"

"Never mind about the dead bear smell!" I cried, my eyes shining, the thrill of investigation crackling through me, "we have a *prime suspect*! Don't you think?"

"Er, YEAH," Kip said. "*Obviously* he's the prime suspect. We just heard him confess. Mystery solved."

"Not yet!" I said quickly. "We don't have any evidence yet and he's still got Jenny somewhere."

"At least he said that she hadn't been hurt, so we know she's safe," Kip added.

"For now," I replied ominously.

"We'd better get out of here, before we have more explaining to do. . ." Ingrid said wisely.

"And try and find Muggins again," I said. "See if we can uncover any more evidence of where he's keeping Jenny."

We bustled down the corridor until we came to another door, which we threw open, tumbling smack into Mr Grant.

"What are you three up to?" he asked, his eyebrows raised.

"Nothing," I gasped.

"We got lost," Ingrid said at the same time.

"SANDWICHES," Kip yelped. We all turned to look at him. He shrugged. "Er, I mean, we got lost."

"Hmmmmm." Mr Grant didn't look convinced.

"Have you seen Horatio Muggins?" I asked breathlessly.

"No," Mr Grant said, looking confused. "Why?"

"No reason," I said.

"We found his hat," Ingrid explained.

"SANDWICHES," Kip yelped again.

There was a pause and Mr Grant looked at us very carefully, as if weighing up how much trouble we were getting ourselves into. Finally, he said, "OK." Then he turned towards me. "And Poppy, I have something for you – it came in the post this morning." He handed me a large brown envelope. I recognized the handwriting immediately.

"It's from Pym!" I cried, snatching it from Mr Grant's hand.

"But your postcard can't possibly have got there yet," Ingrid said, bewildered. "Why would she write to you now?"

"No, but that's just like her" – I smiled a slightly watery smile – "replying to a letter you haven't even written yet." After all the sadness and anger of the last twenty-four hours I clung to the letter, imagining Pym and the rest of my family's loving faces and feeling a warm glow wrap itself around my heart like a cosy woollen jumper.

"Well you've got a few minutes before dinner if you want to read it," Mr Grant said with a smile.

I was torn. I desperately wanted to read the letter, to feel connected to my family, but I also knew that we needed to track down Horatio Muggins. After all, mystery solving waits for no one! Luckily, I didn't have to make the decision. Ingrid squeezed my arm. "Go and read your letter," she said, and then in a softer voice she added, "We can talk about Muggins later. After all, he said he's not going anywhere."

I flashed her a grateful smile and ran out of the door to find somewhere private to read outside. This was easier said than done as there were lots of students around enjoying their free time in the sunshine and not worrying about solving complicated, mind-bending mysteries, but finally, after locating a quiet spot in the garden, I tore eagerly into the envelope. Inside was a letter, and I recoiled for a moment because it had a rather overpowering smell like the bottom of a slimy pond.

Dear Poppy,

I have been thinking about you all morning and getting the strongest sense that you need to hear from us all. And that trouble is round the corner – the visions are not yet clear, but they tell me that Crumley Castle is a place of many secrets, and I'm sure you won't be able to resist investigating them all. So please look after yourself, Poppy. Just remember to be safe and careful. I am seeing something else now, in my vision, though it is still cloudy. It looks like an old-fashioned pistol? Strange. But perhaps that means something to you. Anyway, I love you so very much, and there are a few people here who would like to add to this letter so I will let them get on with it. Pym xxx

What ho, Poppers!

Hope you are having a splendid time at the old Booth castle. I myself am distantly related to the fascinating Moira Booth, did you know? What a character, eh? I hear she was a whizz at shooting and a real thrill seeker. The old dragon or Great-

Aunt Hortence, as she prefers to be known is rather fond of telling stories about this particular ancestor of ours. I suppose you've heard about her and those smugglers - well, not a lot of people know the whole story on that one and it's a belter, let me tell you! Everything rather good here at the moment. Buttercup sends her great love, of course.

Apologies for the chewed corner!

Luigi

Poppy, I just finished Dougie Valentine and the Hamster Wheel of Catastrophe — what a masterpiece! Is it the best one yet? Maybe. We are all well, though there has been a very small mishap with a bottle of perfume that hardly needs repeating

BAH! TOMATO. I TELL MARVIN HE MUST TELL YOU OF HIS BETRAYAL HIMSELF BUT HE IS MAKING MESS OF IT SO I SHALL TAKE CHARGE AS USUALS. HE HAS RUINED MY VERY NICE EXPENSIVE PERFUME. IT USED TO SMELL OF ROSES BUT THEN MARVIN HE WAVE HIS WAND AROUND LIKE NINCOMPOOP AND NOW IT IS GREEN AND SMELLS OF THE SLUDGE. WHO WANTS TO SMELL LIKE THE

SLUDGE, I ASK YOU? HE SAYS IS ACCIDENT
BUT I THINK WE ALL KNOW THAT WHEN HE
LET THAT OCTOPUS STEAL MY EARRINGS

That was ONE TIME and it was years ago and I don't
appreciate you bringing all of this up in what is
SUPPOSED to be a nice letter to Poppy.

SORRY IF THE LETTER IS NOW STINKY,
TOMATO. I SPRAY MARVIN IN THE FACE
WITH SLUDGE PERFUME. IS TASTE OF HIS
OWN MEDICINE, BUT ACTUALLY, BECAUSE
SOME SPRAY WENT INTO HIS MOUTH
HOLE. I THINK HE IS NOW BEING SICK. IS
HILARIOUS. I HOPE YOU ARE NOT BEING
EATEN BY THE SHARKS. FANELLA XXX

I folded the letter up carefully, holding it well away from my nose. It had given me a lot to think about, and not just the fact that I missed my crazy circus family. Pym's vision of the old-fashioned pistol was interesting. Was it connected to Moira Booth? After all, Luigi did say she was supposed to be an excellent shot. And how come Luigi knew anything about Moira in the first place? Was it possible that he knew more about the smuggler's disappearance? If Luigi had more information, I knew that I needed to get in touch with him, but first there was the small matter of rescuing poor, kidnapped Jenny, catching the despicable Horatio Muggins, and generally saving the day. Not to mention the potential ghost, the tunnels, and the mystery that we had originally been looking into – the disappearance of Henry Redshank. It was, I had to admit, an awful lot to take on – even for a super detective like me.

CHAPTER TWENTY-THREE

Unfortunately my inspiring to-do list was interrupted by the dinner gong. (You know things are serious when that is an unfortunate event!) I joined the stream of students scampering in for dinner and met up with Kip and Ingrid. Over plates of burnt sausages, greasy chips and some nuclear green mush masquerading as peas, I filled them in on the contents of the letter.

"So Luigi might know something about Henry Redshank!" Kip exclaimed.

"And what about Pym's vision?" Ingrid asked. "What do you think that was all about? Something to do with the Redshanks?"

"I don't know." I sighed, frustrated. "Anyway, I think our priority has to be finding Jenny."

"How are we going to do that?" Kip asked, biting into his fourth Cajun-style sausage. "If her mum and dad couldn't find her, how can we?"

"Because we're ace detectives!" I cried. "We need to examine the scene of the crime and look for clues that they've missed. I'm sure we will spot something."

"You mean—" Ingrid began.

"Yes." I nodded firmly. "We need to sneak into Jenny's room. We can do it tomorrow, first thing."

"Or. . ." Ingrid said tentatively. "We talk to Miss Susan again, or Mr Grant. We could tell them what we heard Horatio Muggins saying on the phone."

"No," I barked, not wanting to hear Miss Susan's name or think about her at all. "It's our word against Horatio Muggins's that we overheard him on the phone, and you know they won't take us seriously." I thought back once more to my conversation with Miss Susan and felt the familiar wave of anger crashing over me.

"Are you sure you're OK, Poppy?" Ingrid asked quietly. "Did something happen with Miss Susan?

You've been a bit different lately – even before we came to Crumley. We're both worried about you." Kip nodded in agreement at this.

I so desperately wanted to tell my friends about Miss Susan, but I didn't know how. Especially not now, when Miss Susan had denied that I was her daughter at all.

"I'm fine!" I said, but my voice was coming out all snappy and angry again.

"Sorry, Poppy," Ingrid said. "We're just worried, you seem—"

"I really am fine," I said, trying to change the subject. "And we have a mystery to solve." I waved my arms. "They think we're just kids, they think we can't work things out for ourselves, they treat us like we're idiots, but we can show them! We can prove that we are cleverer than them. We can solve this mystery, and we can rescue Jenny ourselves." My speech was so passionate that it ended with me banging my fist on the table in front of me. Kip and Ingrid still looked a bit worried, but I could tell my stirring speech was winning them round.

"OK," Ingrid said finally. "If you're sure..." I nodded my head. "Then," she continued, "how do we find out where Jenny's room is?"

"We ask Mrs Crockton," I said, spotting her emerging from the kitchen and waving to her.

"Do you need something, duck?" Mrs Crockton asked when she reached us.

"No thanks, Mrs C!" Kip piped up. "Just wanted to say thank you for another top dinner – although, actually if there are one or two sausages going spare, I could probably help out." He peered over Mrs Crockton's shoulder.

"Ahem." I coughed, trying to snap him out of his hungry daze.

Mrs Crockton laughed. "What an appetite you've got!" she said, and Kip looked surprised. "I'll have to watch out for you! Although I have started locking the larder up now." She patted a set of keys that were tied to her apron.

"Not because of me? I wouldn't STEAL food!" Kip was horrified. "I'd just ask for it. Really nicely."

"Oh, duck!" said Mrs Crockton. "I'm sorry, I was only teasing! I know *you* wouldn't steal food, but *someone* was helping themselves to the larder just before you all arrived. Caused me a lot of bother it did with half my ingredients missing, so I had to start locking it up. Now, what can I do to cheer you up? A nice jam split fresh from the bakery perhaps? With some clotted cream?"

"I suppose that MIGHT help," Kip said sadly. "Although probably two would be more effective."

My ears had perked up at this, though. Someone had been stealing food? Was it the same person who was storing tins of food at the beach? But why would anyone be doing such a thing? My mind turned back to the matter of Jenny's room. "Mrs Crockton," I said, interrupting Kip, "I had a question about the castle."

"Yes, dear?" She turned to face me.

"I'm a bit confused about my map," I said, pulling the crumpled sheet from my pocket. "We're doing a bit of research into the buildings history, but it doesn't say how many floors there are. Is it four?"

"That's right," Mrs Crockton nodded. "But most of the rooms are in such a state of disrepair that the family only use the rooms on the first two floors; the second floor for guests, and the rooms on the first floor for the Booths."

"Oh, right," I said, casually.

"Now, shall I go and get those splits for you?" she asked.

"Yes, please!" we chorused.

After all we had a busy day ahead of us the next day and mystery solving was hard work. Best to start stocking up on energizing treats as soon as possible.

The next morning we woke up early, while the others were still all snug in their sleeping bags, so that we could put our plan into motion. The sun was barely up, and the sky was a sleepy golden colour. Ingrid and I met Kip on the castle steps just as he was yawning the biggest yawn in human history.

"Why do we have to do this so eeeearly?" he moaned, stifling another yawn. "I was having the most amazing dream about living in a house made out of chocolate cake..." He trailed off, beaming greedily.

"We have to do it early so that no one will spot us, of course," I said.

"And a chocolate cake house would be completely impractical," Ingrid added.

"When you turned on the taps, chocolate milk came out." Kip's eyes were starry.

"I think we're getting distracted." I said, in my professional detective voice (which I suppose is quite booming and forceful, and left Kip and Ingrid looking a little surprised). "Let's crack on with the case!"

A few minutes later we had crept upstairs to the first floor and were wandering along the long corridor, peeking our heads around as many open doors as we could find.

"Narrowing it down to the first floor was all very well," I grumbled, "but how are we supposed to know which room is Jenny's? This corridor just seems to go on for ever."

"I reckon it's this one," Kip said, coming to a standstill.

"Why?" I asked, making my way over to him.

"Who can say?" Kip said, squinting and stroking an imaginary beard. "But I think this sign saying 'Jenny's Room' was my first clue."

Kip was right, there was a sign on Jenny's door, and underneath it was another one in big red letters. It read KEEP OUT and then underneath that in smaller letters someone had written: THAT MEANS YOU.

"Do you think she knew we were coming?" Kip said, pointing at the sign.

"I'm sure that's for her mum and dad," Ingrid said. "Parents can be so annoying – coming into your room, leaving books about the history of stamp collecting open on your bedside table, putting up posters of rare stamps, changing your alarm clock so that it wakes you up by singing a song of their own composition about the history of perforation and postage stamp separation. . ." Ingrid's cheeks turned a bit pink. Obviously I didn't really have normal parents, but I think these problems were still fairly specific to Ingrid and her mad stamp-collecting parents. (They were bitterly disappointed that Ingrid hadn't followed in their philatelist footsteps.) My assumption was supported by Kip's face, which was looking at Ingrid in total bemusement. "And they try and tidy things up," Ingrid added, and here Kip nodded sagely.

"So if she wasn't talking to us, then what are we waiting for?" I asked. "We know it's not locked because Agatha said they had to break the lock to get in."

The others nodded. Slowly, Kip reached out and turned the door handle.

CHAPTER TWENTY-FOUR

The door swung open and we stepped into Jenny's room. It looked exactly like you might imagine a seventeen-year-old's room to look. And by that I mean it looked as if a clothes shop had exploded. There were clothes and shoes everywhere. A small table with an oval mirror attached to it was littered with make-up and perfume and jewellery. In one corner her bed was rumpled and unmade. The walls were covered in posters of handsome boys and bands with names like Love Connection and BOYCRUSH, whose members all seemed to have floppy hair and big white teeth. There were magazines scattered around and a radio with big speakers stood next to a large wooden wardrobe.

The three of us looked around in silent horror. "Where do we even start looking for clues?" I asked.

"Oh wow, I wish my parents could see this room!" Kip exclaimed. "They're always saying I'm so messy and I keep telling them it could be soooo much worse."

"OK," I said, stepping gingerly around the mess. "We haven't got any time to waste. Let's just do our best and see what we can find."

Ingrid and Kip started rummaging, but I stood

and cast my eye around critically, trying to slip into top detective mode. My eyes ran along the walls, and then along the floor.

"Does that floorboard look right to you?" I asked, pointing next to Jenny's bed. The board in question was a slightly different colour to the others as if someone had mended a gap in the floor a long time ago. I ran over and tapped on it with my foot. The board wobbled. I pushed down harder with my foot on one end, and the other end lifted up into the air. Grabbing on to this, I gently lifted the board away. Underneath it was a small, dark gap.

"What is it?" Kip hollered, stumbling over and throwing himself down, his head over the hole.

"I can't see," I said. "There's a big melon head in the way."

"I do NOT have a melon head," Kip cried hotly, said melon head snapping up so that he could glare at me.

"You've got a very nice head," Ingrid said soothingly. "It's not like a melon at all. More like . . . a football." Kip still didn't look impressed. "A perfectly proportioned football," she added hastily and Kip looked slightly happier.

While this exchange was taking place I had

thrust my hand down into the gap, silently praying that there weren't a family of spiders living down there, and emerged clutching a bundle of envelopes tied with a pink ribbon. "Look!" I exclaimed. "Secret letters!" With fumbling fingers I tugged at the ribbon, loosening it and pulling out the top envelope. The letter J was written on the front in slightly smudged ink. Pulling out the letter inside, I smoothed it on the floor in front of me so that we could all read.

My darling Jenny-kins,

You are so wonderful, you truly make my heart fly. I cannot count the ways in which I love you. I have written you a love poem:

Oh Jenny! You are my heart's desire!
Your skin so soft, your eyes like fire.
You truly are the one I love
For you, heaven and earth I would move.

I hope you like it and that my manly tears haven't smudged the ink too much. I am just overwhelmed by all these emotions. I will meet you in our secret spot tonight at the usual time. Until then, my darling. I love you, always!

XOXOXOXOXOXOXOXOXOXOXOXOXOXOXO
(times one million billion)

"I think. I am going. To puke," said Kip, his face decidedly green. He puffed out his cheeks and clapped his hands over his mouth for added effect.

"That poem is OFFENSIVE to the art of poetry," hissed Ingrid. "What kind of idiot rhymes 'love' with 'move'? There are GREAT words that rhyme with love. Above, glove. . ."

I cut her off here. "Yes, Ingrid, we get it. The poem is pretty shocking." I frowned. "But I wonder who wrote it?"

"DOVE!" cried Ingrid. "My love is gentle as a dove! I mean, it's not rocket science, is it?!"

I was still staring at the letter. A memory was stirring in my mind, but I couldn't work out what exactly it was. "I wonder who they could be from?"

Unfortunately Ingrid was still muttering darkly – I just caught the words, "I mean, *come on*, read a little Shakespeare!" and Kip was still staring at the letter like he was a sailor with a severe case of seasickness. I pulled open some of the other envelopes but it was only more of the same mushy rubbish. None of the letters were signed so there was no clue about who they could be from. With a sigh I tucked the letters carefully in my pocket and gently lowered the board back in place. It was interesting that Jenny had a secret romance – but I couldn't see how that helped us find her kidnappers.

"So, we're no closer to finding out how the kidnapper managed to abduct Jenny from a locked room on the first floor," I said, returning my focus to more pressing matters of mystery. Looking out of Jenny's window I saw nothing but a sheer drop down to the ground below.

"Well, it would be a *lot* easier to search this room if Jenny put *any* of her clothes away," Kip said with a sniff. "I mean, what's even the point of having a wardrobe if you leave it totally empty?" He pointed over to the wardrobe, and I saw that he was right – there wasn't a single item of clothing inside. Not even one.

That struck me as being slightly odd.

I went to the wardrobe and knocked on the sides. Nothing. I climbed inside and tapped on the back. Still nothing. With a sigh I clambered down. "Thought I was on to something there," I muttered.

"Maybe you were," said Ingrid, her big owl-like eyes blinking behind her glasses. "Maybe the wardrobe *is* hiding something – *behind* it."

"Because having it full of clothes would make it too heavy to move," I said slowly, snapping my fingers.

Without another word the three of us began to push the wardrobe to one side. It moved easily. We stood back, staring at the stone wall.

"Do you think. . ." Ingrid trailed off.

I stepped forward and began pushing gently at the stones. Finally, with a gentle click, one gave way beneath my hand, and the wall slid to one side.

"Well," I said, "I think now we know how the kidnapper got into Jenny's room."

We had found a hidden staircase.

CHAPTER TWENTY-FIVE

We walked down the first couple of steps, and the door slid closed behind us. We were frozen in total darkness. "Errr, did anyone bring their torch with them?" I squeaked, my hands feeling along the cool stone of the wall.

"No," said Ingrid in a trembly voice. "Mine's in the tent."

"I brought mine," Kip yelped, and we all breathed a sigh of relief. There was a fumbling sound and then a clicking noise and then ... nothing. "Ah. Right," Kip said, "I see the problem here. I forgot to change the batteries. So... My bad, you guys."

The darkest darkness smothered us like the

embrace of an over-enthusiastic auntie. "Right," I said brightly. "That's fine."

Kip began to hum nervously. Then: "AGGGGGHHH!" he screeched. "What was that?"

"What?!" Ingrid and I cried in terror.

"THAT HUMMING NOISE!" Kip yelled, "IS IT A GHOST????"

"No, you idiot!" I huffed. "It's *you*."

There was a pause. "Oh right, yeah," Kip mumbled. "Sorry."

"Is it a ghost?" Ingrid repeated angrily. "*You'll* be a ghost when I get my hands on you."

"Rude!" Kip exclaimed. "It's not my fault I hum when I'm being brave."

By now my eyes had adjusted very slightly to the darkness. I could at least make out the two dark shapes that I knew were Kip and Ingrid, as well as the sides of the staircase. "OK" – I took a deep breath – "we can do this. I'm going to feel my way along. Kip, you put your hand on Ingrid's arm. Ingrid, you hang on to me." I began moving slowly forward, inching my feet along the ground as I clung to the rough stonework. Kip began to hum again. Finally, after what felt like an eternity, we reached the bottom of the stairs and what seemed to be a long tunnel. After a few more breath-holdingly tense minutes the tunnel started to get lighter.

"Can you hear that?" Ingrid asked, her head tilted to one side. "It sounds like—"

"The sea!" Kip and I finished, and we all began moving more quickly now towards the noise. And then there was *literally* a light at the end of the tunnel. Daylight, that is. We emerged, blinking, at some rough steps cut into the rock, which we climbed down, on to the sand below.

We were in another cave. This one was much smaller than the other we had found, and much further around to the side of the cove. The tide was just starting to come in and I realized that we had been really lucky – obviously the sea came right in at high tide, filling the cave with water.

"Well," I said, looking around me with satisfaction. "I think we might have solved at least one mystery. Now we know how Horatio Muggins kidnapped Jenny from a locked room!"

We had to rush back to the castle as quickly and with as much stealth as we could muster or we were going to miss breakfast. One look at Kip's face was enough to let me know that such an outcome was *not* going to be acceptable. Luckily, we just managed to slip in with the rest of the group making their way towards the dining hall. I plastered a look of total innocence on my face – one that I felt sure brought to mind the image of a pure and glowing angel.

"My goodness, Poppy. Are you all right?" Mr Grant exclaimed, catching sight of me. "Why are you grimacing like that? Are you in pain?" he asked, quickly reaching for the first-aid kit in his rucksack.

"Oh, no, I'm fine, thanks!" I said, trying to reassure him with the biggest million mega-watt smile I could manage.

Mr Grant blinked. "OK, if you're sure..." he said, before turning to break up a fight between two boys who were shouting about ice cream flavours (I'll let you have a guess who one of the boys was...).

I glanced around but saw no sign of Miss Susan. A wave of relief washed over me. I certainly wasn't ready to face her yet. In fact, I didn't want to see her until I could make her eat her words over my mystery-solving skills. Which reminded me, I had work to do. After scoffing down a bacon sandwich I excused myself to find Mrs Crockton and to ask very nicely if I could use the phone in her kitchen to ring the circus. Kip and Ingrid hung back in the dining room to give me some privacy as I lifted the handset and dialled the number. I needed to talk to Luigi and find out what this extra info he had about Moira Booth and the smugglers was.

Begin Transcript

Cheery Baz: All right? Booming Badger 'ere.

Me: Hello, Cheery Baz! It's me.

Cheery Baz: (big sigh) Oh. You. Again.

Me: Yes, listen. I need to talk to Luigi; it's important.

Cheery Baz: Oi! Luigi! It's What's 'er name on the phone for you!

Luigi: (in the distance) Lord Wassername, did you say? Good lord, haven't heard from him since we were young pups. Rufus, old chum! Is that you?!

Me: No, Luigi, it's me.

Luigi: Poppers? Good Gad, why are you impersonating Old Rufus Wassername?

Me: I'm not. But I need to talk to you. It's about Moira Booth.

199

Luigi: Ahhhh! Of course. At Crumley Castle, aren't you? Finally got a telephone installed, have they? I think we had to communicate by carrier pigeon last time we were there. (honking laugh) Ada Booth just hated anything new-fangled – great friends with Hortence, of course.

Me: Yes, they've had a phone installed, but I—

Luigi: Poppers, before I forget I must tell you about what Buttercup did yesterday—

Doris: (in background) Did you say Poppy's on the phone?

Scuffling noises

Doris: Poppy! We got your postcard. Now, about this locked room mystery. . . I have some questions.

Me: Yes?

Doris: First of all: did the person who disappeared have access to high-powered lasers?

Me: No.

Doris: Any kind of nuclear facility?

Me: No.

Doris: Did he have the skills to construct a robot arm with seven moveable fingers?

Me: I don't think so, DoDo. He was a smuggler in the eighteenth century.

Doris: Ah. (Pause) Tricky. Are you sure he went into the room? The easiest way to disappear someone is if they were never there in the first place.

Me: Lots of people saw him go into the room, and they heard him arguing with someone inside. There's nowhere else he could have slipped away before locking himself in. It's a real mystery!

Doris: Hmmmm. Sounds like the perfect disappearing act to me! I'll have to put my thinking cap on. . .

Scuffling noises

Luigi: Yes, *thank you*, Doris. Poppy and I were actually having a very important conversation.

Me: That's right. Luigi—

Luigi: So Buttercup did the most adorable thing—

Me: LUIGI! I need to talk to you about something important. Moira Booth! You said that Great-aunt Hortence told you all about her.

Luigi: Oh yes, the old dragon! She has a real soft spot for Moira Booth... Some great-great cousin twice-removed or some such. But I have to admit she sounds a fascinating woman. Very handy with a gun she was, and practically a pirate you know.

Me: A pirate?

Luigi: Oh yes, so the tale goes. You've probably heard the stories about the smugglers down there. Brothers, they were. I can't remember the names now...

Me: The Redshank brothers!

Luigi: That's it, yes. Kept getting away with all sorts of mischief, and no one knew how, but that's because the magistrates didn't suspect they had help from a wealthy benefactor.

Me: You don't mean...

Luigi: Oh yes, she sent the customs officers

202

on a merry dance – none of them suspected
a rich young lady like her!

Me: Wait, Moira Booth was working *with* the
smugglers?!

Luigi: Not *with* them, Pops. They were
working *for* her. She was in charge of the
whole operation by all accounts. The old
dragon has simply heaps of stories about
Moira Booth that I'm sure she'd love to
share next time we visit Burnshire Hall.
You know what she's like when she gets
the bit between her teeth, and a story
going – can't get her to stop waffling on
and on and on and on. I remember when I
was a youth—

Me: Yes, very interesting. I can't believe
that Moira was in on the smuggling! How
does Great-aunt Hortence know this?

Luigi: Oh, stories getting passed down, you
know. The legend of Moira Booth was one
I heard as a tiny lad at the knee of my
great-aunt, and she from her father before
her, and so on and so on. One doesn't
actually have to go as far back as you may
think given the colossal age of Hortence.

Not actually sure I even know how old she
is. What do you reckon? A hundred and
fifty?

Buttercup: ROOOOOOOOAR!

Luigi: Oh, Poppers! My little Buttercup is
here to say hello! (makes kissy baby face
noises)

Sound of Buttercup purring loudly

Sound of door banging

Fanella: LUIGI! THAT PIG-LION OF YOURS IS
CHEW ON MY HAIRBRUSH AGAIN!

Luigi: How DARE you besmirch Buttercup like
that! She is VERY well behaved. She doesn't
chew on anything.

Fanella: YOU BONE HEAD! SHE CHEW ON THE
PHONE CABLE RIGHT N—

Phone goes dead

End of Transcript

I put the phone down in a state of shock. *The Redshank brothers were working for Moira Booth!* I turned the story that we knew over in my mind. I thought about the events of that fateful night, which I now saw in a very different light. Moira must have helped Henry Redshank to escape somehow, I realized. This also meant that Henry could have used the tunnel from the beach to the library because it wouldn't have mattered that Moira was in the room. But why had he come up to the castle at all? Perhaps it was to warn Moira that the customs officers were on the warpath? So why leave the library at all, then? After all, the cook said she bumped into Henry in the hallway. My head was spinning with questions.

At that moment Kip and Ingrid burst into the room, and I filled them in on Luigi's revelations.

"Wow," Kip blew out a big breath he'd been holding. "So Moira Booth was Henry Redshank's accomplice all along. Do you think she hid him somewhere?"

"I don't know," I admitted, "but I think we need to get another look around in Agatha's study to see if it's a possibility."

"But the customs officers tore the room apart,"

Ingrid pointed out. "Moira Booth may have been in on it, but we have no idea how she made a man disappear completely. Maybe she knew how to do magic tricks – just like your family, Poppy."

Something was rattling alarm bells in my brilliant detective brain, but I had no time to grab on to the idea that was forming because just then Mr Grant stuck his head around the kitchen door.

"There you are!" he exclaimed. "Come on, it's surfing time!"

CHAPTER TWENTY-SIX

When we started our surfing lesson I was busy mulling over the new information about Moira Booth, but even these exciting matters of mystery were chased out of my head by the exhilaration of being on a surfboard. Running into the waves at full pelt and battling against the icy water was exhausting and great fun. I was definitely no pro, but I managed to get up on my board a couple of times, and in the end it didn't really matter... What mattered was that, for a glorious hour, I was not thinking about Miss Susan, I wasn't thinking about Jenny or the smugglers. My mind was as smooth and uncomplicated as a tub of vanilla ice cream.

Nearby, Kip was bouncing around in the water

like an excited puppy, but Ingrid didn't seem to be having the best time. For one thing, she couldn't wear her thick glasses while she was in the water, so she was currently as blind as a bat. For another thing, Ingrid's coordination wasn't great at the best of times, but add in the blindness and there was a lot of tripping and bumping going on.

It was right at the end of the lesson that Annabelle decided to take advantage of this. Ingrid was wobbling about in the shallows, trying to keep hold of the bodyboard that was attached to her wrist by a Velcro strap, when I saw Annabelle sidle over.

"Having some trouble there, are we, Ingrid?" Annabelle asked in her sing-song voice. Ingrid scrunched her eyes up in Annabelle's direction, clearly trying to make out the shape next to her.

"Leave me alone, Annabelle," Ingrid said quietly, before turning to wrestle with her board once more.

Annabelle laughed her stupid flutey laugh. "You're not exactly elegant, are you?" she said in a dangerously sweet voice that I knew meant she was going in for the kill. "You look like a sea lion in that wetsuit, flopping all over the place."

Ingrid didn't say anything, just seemed to concentrate more intensely on trying to lie down on the bodyboard. I was already making my way over to them when I saw Annabelle reach out and give Ingrid's board a good tug. The board flipped over with Ingrid beneath it, pushing her under the water. I watched in horror as Annabelle laughed while Ingrid kicked and splashed, until one of Ingrid's long legs booted Annabelle in the backside, knocking her into the water as well. Annabelle immediately began shrieking like a banshee.

My heart was pounding but in the split second before I could pull Ingrid out of the water myself, I saw two strong, tanned arms lift her into the air. Jack Jenkins carried a coughing and sputtering Ingrid back to the sand where he set her gently on the ground. All of this was watched by a crimson-faced Annabelle, who had emerged from the water, her blonde hair hanging around her face in soggy rats' tails. The look in her eyes was one of fury. Her pal Barbie appeared at her side making sympathetic clucking noises, but Annabelle angrily shook off her comforting hand.

"Thank you," Ingrid wheezed up at her rescuer.

"No problem." Jack smiled, his hair flopping into his eyes. Ingrid turned a bit pink and even I had to admit that Jack was pretty dreamy. I huddled in the sand next to Ingrid with my arm around her shoulder.

"Are you OK?" I asked.

She nodded. "I just feel like an idiot," she mumbled.

"It wasn't your fault," I said fiercely. "You were doing great. It was the terrible Annabelle, as usual. I wish Fanella was here... She'd want to put Otis the snake in Annabelle's sleeping bag, and I would NOT stop her."

Ingrid giggled weakly and leant against my shoulder. I felt something warm spreading through my chest. It felt like a long time since I had been this relaxed with my best friend. It was nice.

Unfortunately, the nice moment was cut short by the appearance of Jack's girlfriend. She stared down at Ingrid and me with obvious disdain. "Jack, are you nearly finished with these *kids*?" she sulked, the word "kids" was spoken like a dirty word. "We were *supposed* to be spending the day together."

Jack wrapped his arm around her shoulder. "I'm sorry, my little Betsy-kins," he murmured gently. "But we're nearly done, and you know I can't turn down the work." He gave her a tiny wink. "And I can use the money to buy you something nice."

Betsy was still pouting, but her voice had softened when she said, "All right then, but you owe me!" She turned and stomped off with a toss of her head.

Jack grimaced at us. "Looks like I'm in the dog house!" he said ruefully, and then he grinned, and I smiled back, thinking he was way too good for this Betsy girl. There was something about her that was bothering me, but I couldn't quite put my finger on what it was.

The surfing lesson was well and truly over by now, and we headed up to the castle for lunch. When we arrived there seemed to be a bit of a commotion outside on the front lawn. Bernard Booth was standing with his arm around a weeping Agatha, and he was shouting at Fuddling who remained as stone-faced as ever.

"How could you not have seen anything?" Bernard yelled. "You're supposed to be keeping an eye on things. I can't believe that this has happened again."

Agatha was sobbing gently and Mr Grant jogged over, a concerned look on his face. I tried to sidle over as stealthily as possible so that I could find out what was going on. My heart quickened; was this something to do with Jenny's disappearance?

"What's going on?" Mr Grant asked. "Is everyone all right?"

"We're fine," Bernard said wearily. "It's those vandals again, they've been playing about with the spray paint." He gestured towards the shiny new bathroom conversion for the camping site. There, on the side, the word LEAVE had been scrawled in red paint.

"Who would write such a horrid thing?" whispered Agatha.

"The same idiots who put a brick through the window last week," said Bernard, with a scowl. He turned to Fuddling again and pointed an accusing finger at him. "And you told me you would keep an eye on things."

"With respect, sir," Fuddling said coldly, "I have only one pair of eyes and I cannot be everywhere at once. As I suggested before, you would be wise to employ some sort of groundsman for the purpose." With this he turned on his heel and swept past us in to the castle.

Bernard Booth was left staring speechlessly after him.

"Let's go and have some lunch," Mr Grant said soothingly. "I'm sure it's just some local kids messing around. We can have it cleaned up in no time." With that he began guiding the Booths back towards the dining hall. We all followed quietly behind.

"What was that about?" Kip hissed out of the side of his mouth.

"I don't know." I shrugged. "Maybe it was the same people who took down all the tents? Someone who doesn't want the Booths here."

"Do you think Muggins did it?" Ingrid whispered.

"Doesn't seem his style," I replied, puzzled. "Although the ransom note did say 'you are not wanted here'."

"But why would Muggins want the Booths to leave the castle?" Ingrid said. "Surely he's just after the ransom?"

"What if it's a ghostly warning?" Kip asked, his eyes widening.

My stomach did a little flip. "I don't think so, Kip," I said with more certainty than I felt. "It probably *is* just someone from the village playing a prank. It's not necessarily related to our cases at all."

The three of us filed into the dining hall and sat down for some lunch. The sea air had certainly given me an appetite and I hoovered up everything in front of me as if my name was Kip Kapur. I think I was beginning to get used to Mrs Crockton's terrible cooking. Once lunch was over we had the whole afternoon to ourselves so while others may have been playing Frisbee in the grounds, or reading in dappled sunlight underneath a tree, Kip, Ingrid and I had work to do. My mind was positively spinning with things we needed to get on with. Top priority was going to be finding where Muggins was keeping Jenny. We now knew how he had kidnapped her from her locked room, and we knew that she was safe and that he was staying put for the time being thanks to the phone call we had overheard, but we still didn't know where he had stashed her while waiting for his ransom demands to be met. It seemed likely that if Muggins was hanging around then Jenny must be somewhere nearby.

There was also the matter of Moira Booth. Now that we knew she had been working with the vanishing smugglers, their disappearance was even more intriguing. To be completely honest with you, I wasn't sure what our next move should be. As we finished our lunch I saw Kip and Ingrid looking at me expectantly and realized that I was going to have to come up with some sort of a plan, and pronto.

"So. . ." I said, remaining in my seat as the other

students left the hall and hoping that if I started saying words then a plan would miraculously fall from my lips. "I've been thinking about a plan and planning for what we should do next, and the mystery of it all is so, you know, *complex*. . . but that's not to say it's unsolvable, as long as we have a plan, which I do. Have a plan. Definitely. Because making a plan is an important thing to do. And so the plan is. . ." I had been talking for a long time without taking a breath, and I could see Ingrid and Kip's eyes getting rounder and rounder.

"Poppy?" a voice was at my shoulder and I turned to see Mrs Crockton's smiling face.

"Hello, Mrs C!" I cried, overjoyed that I didn't immediately have to present my top-notch plan to my friends. Mrs Crockton, I saw, was beaming all over her face and wobbling a bit like a jelly with suppressed excitement.

"If you three would like to come with me," Mrs Crockton said mysteriously, "there's someone you might like to meet."

We followed her into the kitchen where we found an old man sitting in one of the chairs. He was very tanned and wrinkly, with wispy grey hair, and his right eye was all scrunched up. He held an unlit pipe in his left hand and, despite the warmness of the day, he was wearing a raincoat and a pair of thick black boots.

"Children," Mrs Crockton said, "Allow me to introduce you to . . . Tom Redshank."

CHAPTER TWENTY-SEVEN

The three of us stood as though turned to stone. Had Mrs Crockton really just said this man was Tom Redshank?

"G-g-ghost smuggler!" stuttered Kip, his face pale and his eyes bulging like currants in a Chelsea bun.

Tom Redshank laughed a low, rumbling laugh. "Afraid not, little 'un. I'm as real as the day is long."

Kip bristled at the "little" comment, but given that we had yet to establish how dangerous the man – or spectre – in front of us was, he kept his mouth shut in a thin line.

I had to admit that I was inclined to believe the man was no ghost. For one thing he looked very alive, and for another I didn't think that ghosts wore yellow rain macs.

"Tom here is distantly related to the Tom Redshank you know about," Mrs Crockton clucked. "I ran into him in the village and mentioned that you were interested in the stories of the Redshank brothers. Thought you might like to hear about it all from the expert." She smiled at us and I could feel my own mouth spreading into an answering grin. Had Mrs Crockton just delivered us a new line of enquiry when my plans had reached a dead end? I wanted to do a little jig right there and then.

"Anyway," Mrs Crockton continued, "I must just go and check on the laundry. I'll leave you four to get acquainted. There's tea in the pot there. Would you like some biscuits?" she asked.

There was a pause. "Er... Made 'em yourself did you?" Tom asked shrewdly.

"No, I didn't have time," Mrs Crockton sighed. "I've been that busy."

"What a shame," murmured Tom, meeting my eye so that we could share a look of great relief. "Biscuits would be lovely, Mrs C ... though not a patch on yours, of course."

"Get away with you!" A pleased blush spread over

Mrs Crockton's cheeks and she plonked a biscuit tin on the table before bustling out of the room.

Tentatively the three of us sat around the kitchen table with Tom. He poured us all cups of tea then sat back, his unlit pipe in his mouth. "Well then," he drawled, "I hear you lot have some questions, do ye?"

I nodded, my mind racing. Where to begin?

"We heard the story of Henry Redshank's disappearance and it sounded really interesting," Ingrid began carefully. "We are interested in mysteries, and this seemed like a good one."

Tom nodded. "Oh yes, it's a good one all right. Puzzlin' people for over two centuries as it's been."

"Do you believe in the ghost?" Kip blurted out, sending a mouthful of biscuit crumbs spraying across the table. "Do you believe that he's still here in the castle, I mean?"

Tom raised one eyebrow but didn't speak for a moment. "I know there are a lot of goings-on up here," he said, eventually. "Goings-on that can't be easily explained." He sat back in his chair and sucked thoughtfully on his pipe. "But do I believe this hokum about deals with dark forces?" He shook his head. "No, I do not."

"Did you know that Moira Booth might have been

working with the smugglers?" I asked quickly.

Tom looked at me from under bushy white eyebrows. "Ah," he said softly, "I heard a rumour or two in that direction. Doesn't surprise me, from what I hear about Moira Booth."

"Like what?" Kip asked, reaching for his third biscuit.

"Oh, she was quite the firecracker, so the stories go." Tom smiled. "Expert fencer, crack shot – could hit a moving target from a mile away, that sort of thing. Even heard she knew how to box, if you can believe such a thing of an eighteenth-century gentlewoman."

I could. The more I heard about Moira Booth the more excellent she sounded. "So it really does sound like she could have been helping the Redshank brothers, even leading them?" I said slowly.

There was another pause and the pipe was returned to Tom's mouth. "Well, now, here's where we run into problems, see," he muttered. "All this talk of the Redshank brothers is strange indeed."

"Why's that?" Ingrid asked with a frown.

"Well, it's like this," Tom said. "Tom Redshank was a smuggler and no mistake. After that night he sailed to France and lived a good life by all accounts, falling in and out of trouble." Here Tom fell silent for a moment, glancing around the table at all three of us, making sure he had our attention. "There is one strange thing though," he said finally. "I've been through the family tree a dozen times, and Tom Redshank didn't have no brother."

"What?" I gasped.

Tom nodded.

"Well…" Ingrid frowned. "Maybe Tom and Henry were cousins or something and people at the time got it wrong and thought they were brothers and it stuck?"

"Well that makes sense," Kip said. "It's just that over time people have started referring to them as brothers instead of cousins."

Tom leant back in his chair again. "Could be," he said with a smile. "But I can't find any cousin in the family tree either."

A crackling silence filled the room.

I finally broke the atmosphere. "What … what exactly are you saying?" I asked.

Tom's eyes met mine. "I'm saying that *whoever* Henry Redshank claimed to be, he weren't no Redshank." He waved his pipe at me again. "I'm saying there never was no Henry Redshank to begin with."

We were interrupted then by the return of Mrs Crockton, her arms full of clean laundry. "Everything all right in here?" she asked.

I couldn't speak, and neither it seemed could Kip and Ingrid. Tom stretched and got to his feet. "It's fine," he said. "Always nice to have a chat about the family history, but I'd best be off." He moved towards the door. "Thanks for the tea," he said to Mrs Crockton before turning to us, "And good luck with the investigation. It's a head-scratcher, that's for sure." He gave a low chuckle and with that he was gone.

My head was spinning. The further into this mystery we got, the more complicated things became. Who was the mysterious man that we knew as Henry Redshank? Something was tugging at my mind – the solution to this problem was so close I could almost touch it.

Mrs Crockton must have noticed our dumbstruck faces. "Are you all right?" she asked, her voice full of concern.

I was about to answer, when a terrible sound split the air.

Someone was screaming.

CHAPTER TWENTY-EIGHT

All four of us ran in the direction of the awful scream – it was coming from the drawing room. When we arrived, we saw Agatha, limp and crying in the arms of her husband. Mr Grant was standing nearby, a stunned look on his face. Fuddling was also there, but his face remained as emotionless as ever.

"Agatha! My dear! What is it? What's wrong?" Mrs Crockton asked breathlessly.

"It's Elaine!" Agatha said in a quavering voice, and a shiver of fear ran through me. "She's been ... kidnapped!"

Miss Susan – kidnapped? I had to lean against the back of a nearby sofa, as my knees seemed to have turned to the wobbliest of jelly.

"What?" Mrs Crockton gasped.

It was then I noticed Mr Grant was holding a piece of paper in his trembling hand. I took it from him gently. He didn't even seem to notice. It was another ransom note. I handed it to Ingrid who read it aloud:

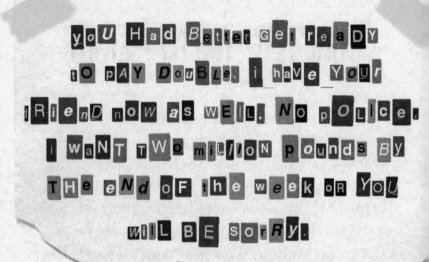

yoU Had Better Get reaDY tO pAY DouBle. i haVe Your iRienD noW as WEll. No pOLIce. i waNT TWo miLlION pounds By THe eNd OF the week oR YoU wiLL BE soRRy.

"What is going on?" Mrs Crockton was looking wildly around at the other grown-ups. "Is this real? And what does it mean: 'I have your friend *as well*'?"

"As well as Jenny," choked Agatha miserably. "Jenny was kidnapped four days ago." Her voice was barely above a whisper.

Mrs Crockton turned deathly pale and sat down hastily in the nearest chair. Even Fuddling looked shocked.

"What happened, exactly?" Ingrid asked in a voice that sounded like it was coming from far away. "When did Miss Susan disappear?"

Agatha was crying again. "I don't know!" she wept. "I don't know how it happened – it seems impossible. I hate this place! Something wicked is at work here!"

"What do you mean, it seems impossible?" I asked urgently, my brain beginning to whirr back into action.

"We . . . we were having a drink in here," Agatha explained through her sniffles. "We were talking about Jenny. Elaine said that she was going to call an inspector she knew – someone who we could trust to help us. She'd been trying to get me to agree since she found out about the kidnapping and she finally wore me down. I agreed that she should contact him."

"Inspector Hartley," Kip said.

Agatha nodded. "Elaine was just going to phone him," she continued, "and then Fuddling came to talk to me – he said that someone had broken another window." All eyes swung towards Fuddling and he nodded slightly. "I didn't want him to overhear the phone call, so I took him out to the hall. We spoke for five minutes and when I came back, Elaine was ... gone! And that," she pointed a quivering finger towards the note, "was in here instead. But we were in the corridor!" she insisted, "and no one came in or out of the room!"

Mrs Crockton exclaimed in horror, clutching her chest, and Fuddling nodded slowly. "It's true," he said in his flat voice. "Miss Susan did not leave this room. We would have seen."

"No you wouldn't!" I exclaimed. Everyone turned to me. Without another word I made my way over to the secret door.

I had been wondering and wondering whether this tunnel could have been opened from this side and now I was sure – there was no other way Miss Susan could have vanished. But how did you control the door? I noticed one of the stuffed deer heads that was mounted right next to where the door had been. It was then I realized one of the antlers was a little bit crooked. "Kip, give me a boost!" I said.

Kip threw himself forward, a heroic look on

his face as he cradled his hands and puffed out his chest. (He was always happy to show off how strong he was – it came in very handy whenever you needed someone to help chuck you in the air.) I put one foot in Kip's hands and he threw me up as hard as he could. Somersaulting towards the wall I reached out and grabbed on to the deer's right antler. With a creaking noise I felt it move in my hand and then spring back into place. Silently, the secret door slid open revealing the dark tunnel behind. I turned back to see the flabbergasted faces of all the grown-ups staring at me. "There's a secret tunnel," I said unnecessarily. "That's how someone could take her out without you knowing."

"How – how did you find this? How could we not know that was there?" Bernard Booth cried. He swung around to face Fuddling. "Did you know about this?"

"No!" Fuddling's shocked face told me that he was telling the truth. "I had no idea . . . not in all my years here. I swear."

"But you would have heard something." Mr Grant seemed to be waking up now. "Elaine wouldn't go without a fight. If someone had tried to kidnap her, she would have made a commotion."

"Not if she was knocked out first," I said, my eyes landing on another important clue. I walked over to the drinks table where a small glass sat, half filled with amber liquid.

"What's this?" I asked Agatha, pointing to the glass.

"It's Elaine's drink," she said. "The sweet sherry she likes. I got it for her specially . . . she's the only one who drinks it. . ." She trailed off in horror. "You think someone drugged her drink?" she gasped again.

"I think *somebody* knew that she was the only one who drank sweet sherry," I said, feeling all the pieces of the puzzle falling into place. "It would be easy to put something in the bottle."

Agatha let out a little sob. "You're right, she was woozy just now. I told her she needed to have a lie down, but she shrugged it off. I thought it was the stress of all this. Goodness knows I've been feeling it too!"

"If someone put something in her sherry to knock her out it would be easy to overpower her. She might even have dropped off before the kidnapper made his move!" I exclaimed.

"But why would anyone want to kidnap Elaine?"

Bernard asked, his hands spread in front of him.

And then, with perfect timing, Horatio Muggins appeared on the scene. Alongside him were Stanley Goodwill and Jack Jenkins. Horatio certainly didn't look like he had just pulled off a daring kidnap. His dark suit was as neat as ever, not a stitch out of place. However, he brought with him a familiar musty smell that I couldn't quite place.

"What's all the commotion?" he asked in his deep, rumbling voice.

"Jenny and Miss Susan have been kidnapped!" Mrs Crockton burst out before anyone could say anything.

Stanley Goodwill and Jack Jenkins both looked shocked. I watched Horatio's face very carefully. It was difficult to know what he was thinking.

"But – but that's awful. Just awful!" Stanley Goodwill fretted, his pale watery eyes bulging. "Why would anyone kidnap them?" He turned to Jack as if looking for answers. Jack turned to Horatio who remained as still as a statue.

"It's a ransom demand," Bernard said bitterly, his eyes flickering towards Horatio Muggins. "Someone seems to think we have access to two million pounds."

Horatio frowned.

"We're not supposed to tell anyone!" Agatha screeched hysterically. "We shouldn't be talking about it. What if the kidnapper hurts them?"

"Who would do a thing like this?" Jack Jenkins asked, glancing around the room as though looking for any clue.

"An excellent question," I said, and Kip and Ingrid came to stand either side of me. "And one that I think we know the answer to." I looked at Kip and Ingrid, who both nodded. This was the right moment. "The game's up, Horatio Muggins! We know you kidnapped Jenny and Miss Susan. Now tell us where you've hidden them!"

CHAPTER TWENTY-NINE

"What?!" There was a collective gasp and everyone's eyes swivelled to Horatio's face. He looked surprised and angry – probably upset that three kids had wrecked his scheme to nab two million pounds.

"What are you talking about?" he asked, roughly.

"Ahhhh! You deny it?" I cried, really getting into the role of a detective revealing her solution to the mystery.

"Deny what?" he snapped menacingly. "Kidnapping? Yes, as it happens, I do."

"What – what are you talking about, children?" Agatha stuttered. "You think that Mr Muggins had something to do with this?"

"We don't *think*!" exclaimed Kip. "We know!"

"We overheard him," Ingrid said nodding.

"There's no wriggling out of this one, Muggins," I said, doing my best Dougie Valentine impression. "Your goose is well and truly cooked!"

"My goose?" Muggins looked really confused now, and I worried that he wasn't playing his part very well. In Dougie Valentine when the criminal is accused they get angry and reveal their whole evil plot. "What are you lot on about?" Muggins said instead, scratching his head.

"We heard you on the phone," I said, a little less confidently now. "You said you were going to get the money from the Booths, that they had no choice but to agree to your terms. We know that you're the kidnapper! But you won't get away with it on our watch!" I folded my arms, striking a triumphant pose, and Kip and Ingrid followed suit.

Horatio Muggins rubbed his hand over his face. "Well, this is what you get for listening in to other people's conversations that don't concern you," he said finally. "I'm NOT a kidnapper. I work for a bank."

"What?!" I yelped.

Agatha and Bernard were nodding wearily. "It's true, Poppy," Agatha said. "We didn't want everyone to know because we were embarrassed, but we borrowed a lot of money from the bank to renovate parts of the castle and the campsite." (Me, Kip and Ingrid already knew this fact, of course, but only through listening in on *another* private conversation between Miss Susan and Agatha in her study and so I thought it best to pretend that this was brand-new information.)

"This is brand-new information," I said loudly.

Agatha gave me a funny look, but continued. "The bank sent Horatio to stay with us for a couple of weeks to oversee the project, and to determine if the castle was worth further investment."

"Which it is, by the way," Horatio added, with just a ghost of a smile. And for a second Agatha and Bernard looked almost happy, until they remembered what was going on. "So I'd be the last one to make ransom demands," he said. "I knew that the Booths didn't have that sort of cash, in fact I was trying to get them an extension on their loan so that they'd have the time to get the campsite up and running."

"But . . . but you made a threat," I said desperately. "You said that no one had been hurt yet, but that they had to take it seriously!"

Muggins looked puzzled for a moment, then his brow cleared. "I was talking about health and safety regulations," he said. "We need to make sure everything's bang up to code."

I was stunned. *Horatio Muggins was innocent!*

"But what about the inheritance?" Fuddling burst out suddenly, startled out of his usual stoney-faced silence.

"There *is* no inheritance," Bernard replied, "just the castle and a whole heap of bills."

"So Ada Booth ... lied to me?" Fuddling murmured.

"And it serves you right, you old grump," Mrs Crockton snapped. "You ought to be ashamed of the way you've been sulking around."

Fuddling really did look ashamed now. "I'm sorry, sir, madam," he said with a little bow towards Agatha and Bernard. "I thought you were withholding my own inheritance from me, I thought you were being stingy, not hiring any extra help. I didn't realize..."

"Oh, Fuddling." Agatha sighed. "I wish you had said something sooner. We would never do anything like that!"

"I see that now, madam." Fuddling was going a bit pink around the edges. "I apologize."

"Well, this is all very interesting," said Mr Grant, his voice taut and anxious, "but we're no closer to finding out who has Jenny and Elaine." He turned to Agatha. "I know you're scared, but I think now it might be time to call in the police."

"Oh, but we can't," Agatha wailed. "What if the kidnapper hurts them?"

"Yes," Jack Jenkins cut in, "if the note says no police, then maybe we should do as it says. We don't want anyone to get hurt." There was panic in his voice; he was obviously as shaken as the rest of us.

Mrs Crockton nodded. "It would be terrible to do anything to put them in greater danger," she added.

"But what else can we do?" Mr Grant said, pacing restlessly around the room.

"I can't bear this!" Agatha screeched. "I hate it here, Bernard. I hate this place! As soon as we get Jenny back safely we have to leave. I can't stand to be here for another moment. It's been nothing but misery for us."

Stanley stepped forward and put a hand on Agatha's shoulder. "There, there," he said gently. "You've had a difficult time; you can only do what's best for your poor family."

"We can't just leave, Agatha." Bernard looked anguished. "We've worked so hard. We've invested everything. . ." He was drowned out by the sound of his wife's sobs. Bernard seemed to crumple, and he stared helplessly at his wife. "You're right," he whispered. "Don't worry, Aggie. We'll get Jenny back and then we can leave this place behind."

"But this doesn't help us with our immediate problem," Mr Grant's voice cut through their conversation. "Which is how are we going to track down Jenny and Elaine in the first place?"

I felt my stomach tighten. If Horatio Muggins wasn't the criminal then I didn't know who was. And that meant that I didn't know who had Miss Susan or where they had taken her. My breath started coming in short, sharp gulps.

"Are you OK, Poppy?" Ingrid asked.

"I need to get some air," I whispered.

"We'll come too," Kip replied, but I shook my head. I needed a minute or two to myself.

"I'll come right back," I said. "Don't worry."

With that I ducked out of the room and down the corridor, through the entrance hall and out the front door, where I sat down on the big stone steps, sucking in big lungfuls of fresh, salty air. Outside it was hard to believe it was still sunny, although the early evening air was a little chilly. I shivered. I still felt sick and

236

panicky. What if something happened to Miss Susan? I still had so many questions. I was angry, but that didn't mean I wanted anything bad to happen to her. I felt all muddled up inside like a tumble dryer full of sad and scared feelings. Tears were running down my face, and I didn't seem to be able to stop them.

"Poppy?" I heard Ingrid's voice and turned to see her and Kip standing uncertainly behind me.

"I told you not to come," I said angrily, dashing the tears from my eyes with the back of my hand.

"Sorry, Poppy, we just wanted to see if you were OK . . . and to talk about what we should do next," Kip stammered.

"I don't know what we should do next!" I said, and my voice was trembling. "I don't know what to do. Everything's such a mess."

"Poppy. . ." Ingrid began, reaching out towards me, but I cut her off.

"I'm fine!" I said, panicking as I felt another wave of tears building up inside me. "I'm FINE. Please . . . just leave me alone."

"OK," said Ingrid quietly. "If that's what you want." She turned and left, tugging an uncharacteristically speechless Kip along behind her.

I kicked at the gravel and felt the tears burning

my eyes again. I sat down on the step and pulled my knees up to my chest until I was in a tight little ball, and then I cried big body-shaking cries until there were no tears left in me. What was I doing? How could I be so mean to my best friends? And where was Miss Susan? Where was my mother? Had I really just found her, only to lose her again?

Eventually, when my big tears had turned into snotty, snuffling noises, I came to a decision. It was time to come clean to Kip and Ingrid. None of this was their fault and I just hoped they could forgive me for being so terrible. Together, I knew, we could find Miss Susan and Jenny. We could fix everything.

I took a shuddering breath and stared out across the grounds. Idly I noticed Annabelle in the distance. She was walking away from the castle with a spring in her step. It seemed strange that she looked so carefree when all this craziness was erupting everywhere else.

"What are you crying for?" A sing-songy voice at my shoulder made me jump. "Have you finally realized what a loser you are?"

I swung round, my gaze spinning from her to the figure strolling through the castle grounds. "Annabelle!" I exclaimed. "How can there be two of you?"

Annabelle tipped her head to one side and gave me a long look.

"Is this some sort of trick?" she said, suspiciously. "One of your weird little magic games? Well, not interested, freak."

"No," I gasped, "I just..." I turned to where I had seen Annabelle standing only seconds earlier. Only, of course, it wasn't Annabelle at all. The girl turned and waved. Same ponytail, same clothes... It was Barbie, and Annabelle skipped off to meet her, muttering darkly about weirdos and losers. "Sorry," I called, half laughing and half crying because my feelings were so muddled. "I thought there were two of you, but luckily there's still only one!"

And just like that the final piece of a one-thousand-piece jigsaw of a clear blue sky fell neatly into place. Suddenly, I knew what had happened to Henry Redshank. I knew the truth. "I thought there were two of you, but there's only one," I whispered. I could hear Doris's voice going round and round in my head. *The easiest way to disappear someone is if they were never there in the first place.* Of course there was no Henry Redshank. There never had been, because Henry Redshank *was* Moira Booth.

CHAPTER THIRTY

How had she done it? I wondered. How had Moira Booth tricked them all? Henry Redshank had been her all along, dressing up like a man and having all sorts of swashbuckling adventures with Tom. She must have locked herself in the library that night, pretended to have an argument and shouted through the door in both voices while she took off her disguise and got rid of it somehow. It was genius. But something was nagging at my brain: Pym's premonition about the pistol. How had Moira hidden it? She had definitely had one, but no gun was found in the search of the library so she must have stowed it somewhere. The answer flashed across my brain like the most incredible lightning in a stormy sky. There must have been a secret hiding place in the library. Something small, something just big enough to stow these things way, something no one had found in over two hundred years.

I made my way back into the castle and noticed immediately that the library door was ajar. All the grown-ups were still in the drawing room and I simply couldn't resist. I had to know if I was right. I hurried in and pulled the door firmly shut behind me. Over the fireplace the portrait of Moira Booth watched me with a mischievous twinkle. "You were one seriously cool lady," I whispered, and I could have sworn her almost-smiling mouth turned up even further. "Now where is your secret hiding place?" I stared thoughtfully at the portrait, examining every detail. It was almost, I thought, as though she was looking at something with that secret smile. Perhaps it was silly, but I stood back and followed her eye line. The portrait was looking straight at one of the old, carved bookshelves.

I made my way over and began running my hands over the shelves, looking closely for any sign of a hidden compartment. It was then that I noticed a small knot in the woodwork. Pressing my fingers against it I felt something click and a small drawer opened in the shelf. My heart was pounding. Had I found it? I carefully eased the drawer open and looking inside I caught my breath. What I saw was an old-fashioned pistol and a fragile-looking envelope. As carefully as I could, I gingerly moved the gun aside, and with trembling fingers lifted the envelope gently from the drawer. It felt like tissue paper in my hand. My legs were shaking and I sat down in a nearby armchair, staring at the yellowing paper. I gently opened the envelope and extracted its contents. A letter! When I saw the words written there I felt my heart stutter.

My Darling Tom,

I do not know if there is time to get this letter to you before you set sail. It pains me to know that we will not laugh together over this, our latest exploit, as you will be gone – far away from the blasted customs men, and seeking your fortune and your next adventure on the high seas. How I envy you! Do you think that you may have room for a stowaway? I can tuck my hair into my cap and become a ragged young sailor. We all know I make an excellent boy if the occasion calls for it!

How you would have laughed at my performance last night – I'll never forget old Bidders's face when I ran into her in the hall. I thought everyone would be asleep and I could just slip up to my bedroom and change, but then of course Bidders appeared and called for the customs officer and I had no choice but to go back into the library again. And <u>then</u> having to stage a fight with myself, shouting out in two different voices – I felt a little silly, I can tell you, but it seemed to do the trick.

The worst thing was burning my disguise – they all thought my white shirt was just a nightdress, but I could hardly keep the rest of the gear lying about. The fire was blazing and smoking something rotten and I thought for sure that someone would cotton on, but no one did. How hard it was not to laugh at their astonishment! (Of course there was the problem of my pistol – I could hardly throw <u>that</u> on the fire. . . How fortunate that I had you build that secret drawer for me, my love!) And now I think the Redshank boys really will go down in history. A fitting end to our adventures.

I hope you know that I do not blame you for sailing away. I saw, of course, that you tried to get ashore, and that you made sure I got to the tunnel. My darling, with so many guns on you there really was no other choice – although I know you will have been cursing yourself ever since. I will never forget our time together and the marvellous feeling of being alive. I hope that one day we will meet again.

All my love, always,

Moira

PS – word has reached me that you have already gone. I found your message carved into the tunnel wall. I will keep this letter safe, in the hopes that one day I will deliver it to you myself. Oh! Farewell, my dearest one!

The mystery was truly solved! It all finally made sense now. I felt a smile spreading across my face. What a woman! I definitely had a new hero. Moira Booth was just about the coolest person I had ever heard of. Disguising herself as a man and running around having all these adventures – Brilliant! I wondered if she and Tom Redshank ever met again? As the letter was still in the drawer it seemed unlikely. The thought made me sad.

I looked down at the letter again, and my attention turned to the PS. My detective instincts were kicking in once more. Moira mentioned a message from Tom carved into the tunnel ... but we hadn't found that and I felt certain we would have noticed such a clue. Did that mean... Could that mean ... there was another tunnel? A secret passage that we hadn't found yet! It seemed that the other tunnels had been used in the kidnapping; was it possible that this new one would reveal where Miss Susan and Jenny were being hidden? If so there was no time to lose. Carefully, I returned Moira's letter to its hiding place. I couldn't wait to tell Kip and Ingrid about it later – if they were still talking to me, that is.

I crept from the library, closing the door behind

me and checking that no one was around. The coast was clear. I stood with my hands on my hips. Where could the hidden tunnel be? Unfortunately, I knew the answer was that it could be anywhere in the enormous castle. I almost shouted out in frustration. I was so close to solving this thing, I could feel it. I just knew that our two mysteries were linked together. Now I knew the truth about Moira and somehow I felt as if she had guided me to this second tunnel. Surely I was missing something. It was then that I remembered Mrs Crockton's ghost. That was it! The final clue I needed. There was no way the ghost of Henry Redshank was haunting the castle … not if Henry Redshank was Moira Booth all along. Perhaps Mrs Crockton hadn't seen a ghost disappearing through the wall at all. Perhaps, just like with the disappearance of Henry Redshank, there was a much less supernatural explanation. What if it hadn't been a ghost, but a person disappearing into the secret passageway? Hadn't Mrs Crockton said that the air had got a little colder before the ghost disappeared? Almost as though it was creating a draught by opening a secret door! Moving as stealthily as possible I made my way across the hall to the dining room. A quick look here and in the kitchen revealed that the grown-ups must still be in the drawing room formulating a plan. *Well*, I thought, *hopefully they won't have to worry for much longer.*

Mrs Crockton had seen the ghost through the open kitchen door, so I ran to the wall opposite. I began frantically pressing on the stones there. My blood was pumping and I knew with all of my mystery-solving instincts that I was on the right path. Finally, a small stone moved beneath my fingers and with the tiniest *click* the wall began to slide sideways. If I had had a moustache I would have twirled it right there and then, but I had to make do with a tiny fist pump instead. Staring into the gloom ahead, I knew that all the answers I was searching for lay inside.

CHAPTER THIRTY-ONE

Fortunately, I had learnt my lesson from earlier, and the first thing I had done on returning to the castle was to put my little torch in the pocket of my shorts. I clicked it on and stepped through into the tunnel, the door swinging shut behind me. Straight away I saw something that made my heart skip a beat. Scratched into the side of the tunnel in jagged letter were the words

THANK YOU

And the letters TR and MB carved into a heart.

TR and MB – Tom Redshank, and Moira Booth! It was amazing to finally understand a story that had baffled people for hundreds of years. I traced my fingers over the shallow scrawl. I guess Tom hadn't had a lot of time to write anything more eloquent, what with the customs officers after him and an escape to plan. I shivered as I imagined the scene – easy to do in the cold, dark tunnel that was exactly as it would have been 250 years ago. It was so strange to think that all these people were real people, and not just characters in a story – that they had stood here, scared and hurt. I was glad that Tom had got away, and that Moira had managed to help him. Their story was a real love story, one full of adventure and near-death experiences – all soppy romances should have more of those, I decided.

But for now, I reminded myself, I had a job to do. It seemed as though the secret tunnels we had already discovered had played a part in both Jenny and Miss Susan's kidnapping; was it possible that *this* tunnel was being used by the kidnapper too? If so it must be someone who knew the castle well. I shone my torch ahead of me and made my way carefully along. This tunnel took a steep downward turn, and I felt like I was climbing down into the centre of the earth, mud and dirt sticking to my hands as I tried to catch on to the walls to steady myself. Eventually the ground evened out again and I found that I was in a long passageway with a higher ceiling. Pricking my ears, I could just hear the crashing of the sea again somewhere in the distance. Wherever this tunnel ended up, it was likely to be down by the beach again. I kept on walking, stumbling along on the uneven floor until, suddenly, I was surprised to find a set of wooden steps, more like a very basic ladder, propped against the wall. Shining my torch past the steps, down the rest of the tunnel, then up at the ceiling above them, I realized I had found a trapdoor. *Where*, I wondered, *did that go.* Only I didn't wonder for very long before I was scrambling nimbly up the ladder to find out for myself.

Pushing cautiously against the trapdoor, it creaked open with a dusty thump. I poked my head up through the hole. I seemed to be at the bottom of a spiralling stone staircase. Heaving myself through, I closed the trapdoor behind me and dusted off my hands. I had emerged beside a big, solid-looking wooden door. I tried the handle, but found that it was locked. There was nowhere left to go except up the stairs.

My heart was thundering as I crept up, and up,

251

and up, the narrow steps seeming to go on for ever. What was this place? And what would I find at the top? Finally, I reached the last step and found myself confronted by another heavy-looking wooden door. This time when I tried to turn the handle I felt it move and the door swung open with ease.

What I saw on the other side of the door stopped me in my tracks.

The room I was in was quite large and round; it had a high ceiling with wooden rafters and small round windows. There was some very old bedroom furniture, and another, smaller door at the back that stood slightly ajar and appeared to lead to a very basic bathroom area. There was also a camping stove and next to it, a lot of empty food tins stacked up in a pile. From the window on one wall I could see all the way down to the beach below. I realized that I was in the room at the top of the castle's turret, I must have tunnelled down under the castle and come back up behind the door that blocked it off. But that wasn't the thing that had stopped me in my tracks. No.

The thing that had stopped me in my tracks was the sight of Miss Susan and a girl with long gingery hair. It was Jenny. I had found them!

They were both very pale and seemed to be gagged and tied to the chairs they were sitting on by some kind of thin plastic rope. Otherwise they didn't look like they were hurt.

"I found you!" I cried, beginning to move towards them.

But then, I heard the sound of footsteps below. Thinking fast, I threw myself at the wall, clambering up the rough stonework and stepping out on to one of the wooden rafters as if it were a high wire. Miss Susan's face was turned up towards me and I saw her eyes widen.

Then the door to the turret room opened, and someone walked in. I couldn't quite see them, and so I adjusted my position as silently as possible. When I did catch sight of who it was I had to stifle my gasp. I saw the impossibly blonde hair, the broad shoulders and muscly brown arms. There was no mistaking him – it was Jack Jenkins.

He didn't say very much, just went and checked that the plastic ties were still secure. Jenny was wriggling around in her seat, making muffled noises through the piece of cloth over her mouth. If she didn't stop soon she was going to give me away. I had to make a decision. I had to time it just right.

"Stop it, Jenny," Jack snapped. "Someone will hear you."

I inched along the rafter, my arms out on either side until I was standing directly above Jack. Jenny's wrigglings became more furious.

"Oh, all right," Jack sighed. "I'll take the gag off, but you have to be quiet, OK." He leaned forward and tugged the material. It was now or never.

"Jack!" Jenny shrieked.

I took a deep breath and stepped off the rafter, throwing myself forward into a double somersault and aiming straight for Jack Jenkins.

"Aaaaaaaaaaggggghhhh!" I shouted as I slammed into him, knocking him to the floor with a loud thump. Feeling a bit jangled I got unsteadily to my feet. Jack Jenkins lay out cold on the floor.

I had done it! I had caught the criminal, and saved the day! For some reason Jenny was crying noisily and straining towards Jack's unconscious body. I supposed it was just the overwhelming relief at being rescued.

Rushing over to Miss Susan I pulled the gag away from her mouth, expecting words of gratitude to pour from her lips.

"Poppy, no!" she cried instead, and too late I

heard the footsteps behind me. I started to turn, raising my hands, but something heavy hit me on the head with a sickening crack, and white stars exploded all around me, dancing before my eyes. I felt my knees disappear from under me and then . . . everything went black.

CHAPTER THIRTY-TWO

When my eyes blinked open, it took me a while to remember where I was. My head was really hurting, and in my hazy state I could just hear Miss Susan's voice calling my name over and over again.

"Poppy! Poppy!"

Unfortunately, the more awake I became, the more my head hurt. I also noticed, rather foggily, that my legs seemed to be tied to a chair, and my hands were tied in front of me. *Huh*, I thought, *looks like this rescue mission isn't going quite to plan.*

"Poppy!" I heard Miss Susan's voice again, and turning towards the sound, my eyes came in to focus on her pale, worried face. Next to her was the girl with a frizz of red hair who I had recognized as Jenny. She was crying. And tied to another chair next to me was Jack Jenkins. What was going on?

"I'm OK," I mumbled, and I saw Miss Susan's shoulders slump in relief.

"Well, I'm sure we're all glad to hear that." A sarcastic voice rang out behind me.

I twisted my neck, and my mouth dropped open as a familiar face emerged from the shadows.

It was Stanley Goodwill.

"*You!*" I gasped.

"Yes, me," he said, simply, and it was then that I noticed he held a gun in his hand. My heart sank right down to the soles of my trainers.

"What are you doing, Stanley?" Jack asked, his voice hoarse. "Let me go! I thought we were in this together."

"Well, you thought wrong." Stanley smirked, the gun glinting dangerously in his hand.

"Just let Poppy go, Stanley," Miss Susan pleaded. "She's only a child – she's got nothing to do with any of this."

"Neither of you were supposed to be involved!" croaked Jack from his seat. "If you had both just left things alone, everything would have been fine. No one needed to get hurt."

Jenny was still crying, but she spoke now in a trembling voice. "Jack," she whispered. "I don't understand ... what is going on? This was never part of the plan."

The wheels in my head were turning away. "The plan!" I exclaimed. "You were the one who wrote the love letters to Jenny! Jenny-kins – I heard you call that other girl Betsy-kins. Just like that gross baby talk in the love note."

"What's she talking about?" Jenny's head snapped up. "Does she mean Betsy Johnson? You said there was nothing going on between you!"

"I thought I told you to get rid of those letters!" Jack snarled, ignoring this and turning angrily to face Jenny.

"I couldn't get rid of them, Jacky-Bear!" Jenny wept. "They were so beautiful!"

I snorted at that, and Jack turned back on me. "What?" he said.

"You're not very good at writing poetry." I grimaced.

"I'm sure this is all very interesting," Stanley Goodwill interrupted, "but perhaps you could all stop squabbling and pay attention to the man with the gun."

258

"You'll never get away with this!" I said bravely, but I felt a lot less brave when he raised the gun again. "So," I said, stalling as I looked around, desperate for a way to escape. "The kidnapping was fake." My eyes fell on Jenny tied to the chair. "You all planned it together?"

"Not really," Jenny said miserably. "Me and Jack wanted money to run away together, to start a new life as SOUL MATES." Her eyes were all starry and I had to choke down another snort. "I thought it was Jack's idea to try and get Mum and Dad to part with some of their inheritance money. They were being so stingy with it, they wouldn't let me have any of the things I wanted, or let me go on holiday with my mates or *anything*." Jenny's voice was a bit whiny now. "I mean, I am a Booth, too, you know. That inheritance is, like, mine as well. I didn't know Stanley had anything to do with it. What's he doing here, Jack? What's going on? WHY HAS HE GOT A GUN?" Jenny dissolved into noisy tears.

"Just shut up, Jenny!" Jack snapped. "You've been like this the whole time. I am so sick of you! Are you so thick that you still don't know it was all pretend?!"

"W-what?" Jenny looked stunned.

"I just had to get you to go along with it, so that

I could get the money. Stanley was the one who got me to talk you into it. When the money came through, we were going to split it fifty-fifty, and then I was going to be finished with you. I wasn't about to take you with me... Not when I was going to head off to some tropical island and live a life of luxury." He tossed his bleached hair. "You know I can't be tied down, babe."

Jenny sat with her mouth hanging open. "Wh-what?" she screeched. "How could you?!" She began to struggle in her chair, fire in her eyes.

"Quiet!" hissed Stanley, turning his gun on Jenny who stopped wiggling immediately and gave a scared whimper.

"So it was Jack and Jenny using the smuggler's signals that night?" I said quickly, trying to keep the conversation moving while I came up with a plan. Unfortunately, from the scheming look in Stanley's eyes, he was doing the same. Obviously my arrival had thrown a spanner in the works.

"I had to bring in the food and hide it," Jack was saying. "Jenny signalled that the coast was clear so I could break into the house through the tunnels." He sighed. "I'd been nicking stuff from the kitchen but Mrs Crockton got wise and started locking the larder shut, so I needed another plan."

"So you weren't tied up or anything?" I asked Jenny quietly.

"Only for the last couple of hours," Jenny sniffled. "He said it was to fool Elaaaaaaaine!" She was weeping again now, and I rolled my eyes. Jenny was clearly going to be no help in this crisis and we needed an escape plan for three – maybe even four – people, if we were going to try and save the thoroughly worthless Jack Jenkins from this mess as well. I strained at the ropes on my wrists, but they were tied tight.

"But why did you take me?" Miss Susan asked Jack, her voice betraying only a very slight tremble.

"Yes, Jack, enlighten us," Stanley said now, his voice silky smooth. "Why did you take this woman? The plan was to poison her and shut her up for good. If you had put all of the mixture in her sherry bottle, like I told you, we wouldn't be having this conversation. Why did you take it into that thick head of yours to deviate from the plan?" He was getting louder now, clearly angry and a shiver wiggled down my spine.

"I think I know what happened," I said, sniffing the air and finally placing the musty smell that I had also sniffed when Jack entered the drawing room with Horatio Muggins earlier. "You've been hiding behind that big stuffed bear," I said. "I can smell it on you. You smashed the window so that Fuddling would take Agatha out of the room, then you came back through the tunnel and hid behind the bear, waiting until Miss Susan was alone and unconscious before you grabbed her."

Jack slumped. "I thought it was a really clever plan. I thought you'd be pleased." He turned pleading eyes on Stanley. "If we took her as well then we could ask for more money. It just seemed like such a good opportunity. We didn't really need to get rid of her – no one was supposed to get hurt." He sounded frightened now.

"You were there too, when Horatio Muggins said Miss Susan was the only person who drank the sherry," I said, remembering. "You knew you could hide the poison there."

Jack nodded. "I thought. . ."

"This is exactly the problem," Stanley snapped. "You thought, you thought. . . When will you realize that empty head of yours doesn't contain a single decent idea. This whole thing was my plan all along!"

"Yeah, a great plan," hissed Jack, his own eyes

flashing angrily. "Except now we find out it was all for NOTHING."

"What do you mean?" whimpered Jenny, looking frantically from Jack to Stanley.

"There is no money," I said. "Your mum and dad are broke, Jenny. They couldn't afford to pay the ransom demand." Jenny looked stunned by this – obviously the Booths' secrecy about their money troubles had included their daughter.

"I admit that finding out the inheritance was not all Ada had led me to believe, was something of a blow," Stanley mused aloud, still waving the gun at us. "But then, it was never really my true goal."

"Wh-what do you mean?" Jack looked dumbstruck.

The cogs were whirring away in my brain. "It's about the castle," I said, realization dawning. "You're next in line if the Booths leave... You get the castle."

Stanley's watery eyes shone behind his glasses. "Of course it's about the castle! It's always been about the castle! It's my HOME! MINE!" His hands were shaking now, the gun quivering between his fingers. "I alone appreciated its true history. I loved it, I studied it ... who do you think told Jack about all the tunnels?" He sneered at me. "My research uncovered them years ago."

"So you've been trying to drive the Booths away. You're the one who's been sabotaging the campsite!" I cried.

"The campsite!" Stanley's eyes flashed. "That abomination! Turning this hallowed place of history into some sort of tacky tourist attraction? I couldn't believe it. Such a thing would NEVER happen with me in charge."

"You must have been very angry with Ada when she left the castle to the Booths," I said, desperately tugging at the ropes again.

"Angry?" Stanley let out a short, humourless laugh. "I was furious. After everything I'd done for that old dragon? After all the sucking up for years, putting up with her temper and her nasty little jabs. At least I got my own back on her."

"What do you mean, you got your own back?" I asked, a sinking feeling in my stomach.

"Let's just say Miss Susan here wasn't the first to ingest the poison I had Jack put in her sherry. Though for her there were less ... *fatal* ... consequences."

I gasped. "You don't mean. . ."

"I did what needed to be done," hissed Stanley. "I always do. The castle needs me. I am its protector, its saviour!" He was staring somewhere into the distance, a deadly smile on his face. "And now your interference has left me with a real mess on my hands," he snarled suddenly, waving the gun around in a way that made me feel more than a little bit nervous. "And there's nothing left to do but clean it up and make sure none of you can talk. I'm almost sure the Booths are ready to leave now, but once the kidnapping deadline passes and you don't come back, it will be a certainty ... they won't want to stay in a place filled with such terrible memories. I'll make them hand over what is rightfully mine!"

"What does that mean?" I croaked, tugging desperately at the rope again.

"It means it's time for you lot to go for a little walk."

CHAPTER THIRTY-THREE

Stanley undid the ropes that tied our ankles to the chairs, easily avoiding the desperate kick I lashed out with when he got to me. "That's enough of that!" he said roughly, his eyes sparkling dangerously. He trained the gun on me. "Now stand up, all of you and get down the stairs. No funny business from any of you or I shoot." He smiled a very unpleasant smile and I wondered how I could have ever thought he was a nice old man. "Start walking."

My hands tied in front of me, I walked behind Miss Susan, Jack and Jenny as we made our way downstairs to the trapdoor. *There must be a way out!* my brain cried desperately – but if there was I couldn't see it. At the bottom of the steps Stanley lifted the trapdoor and gestured towards it. "Down you go, and don't forget if anyone tries anything then I start shooting," he said with a smirk. We all clambered down the steps with Stanley behind us once more. Instead of turning back down the tunnel towards the castle, he nudged us in the other direction, towards the sound of the sea. Jenny whimpered with fright and I knew this wasn't good.

The tunnel was getting lighter and the sound of the sea was getting louder as we walked further along. My eyes were straining against the gloom and my brain was working furiously, trying to come up with a plan to get out of there. Finally, we emerged into a familiar cave. "This is where the tunnel from Jenny's room comes out!" I exclaimed.

"Found that one too, did you?" Stanley almost looked impressed. "And here I was thinking I was the only one who knew about the secret tunnels. You can learn a lot if you do your research!"

We were standing at the back of the cave, at the top of another set of rough steps cut into the stone. My heart thudded in my chest, and fear pulsed through me as I realized that the bottom of the cave was filled with water. A small row boat, attached to the cave wall by an old iron chain with a big padlock, bobbed on the waves. Stanley jumped down into the water, surprisingly agile. With the gun still trained on us he forced us to follow. The waves of the incoming tide lapped gently around my ankles.

Taking a key from his pocket, Stanley unlocked the boat and wedged it against the cave wall. Pulling us roughly, one by one he threaded the chain through the loops of rope around our wrists and snapped the padlock shut with a sickening click. The chain was heavy, and it pulled at my arms. I let out a whimper of fright.

Stanley pocketed the gun. He didn't need it any more, not now that we had so helpfully chained ourselves to the seabed. With a sickening smirk he clambered into the row boat and gave us a little salute. "I'm sorry it had to end like this," he said. "I'll be sure to comfort your parents, Jenny, as I'm helping them pack their bags! What a shame none of you will ever be seen again. Goodbye!" And with that he rowed quickly out of the mouth of the cave, disappearing from sight.

We were alone. The roar of the water bounced off the walls of the cave and I gulped. The water was nearly up to my knees. I was trying not to panic but

I could feel fear rising inside me as fast as the water was filling the cave.

"We're going to diiiiiiiiie!" Jack screamed, which I had to admit did not help my attempts to remain calm.

"Shut up, Jack!" Jenny snapped. "This is all your fault!" It seemed safe to say that their romance was well and truly over.

"Be quiet, both of you," Miss Susan said sharply. "No one's going to die. We just need a plan." She was tugging at the ropes around her hands. "And Stanley Goodwill doesn't know that I phoned Inspector Hartley this morning – I was having a hard time persuading Agatha so I just went ahead and did it without telling her. One way or another people are going to work out what's happened, and your bickering is not helping."

For some reason I found Miss Susan's crossness reassuring. I began to take stock of the situation – *after all*, I reminded myself as the water rose around me, *you've been in worse situations*. I wasn't so sure this was true, but I told myself it was all the same. There was no sense in being defeatist. If anyone could get us out of this mess it was going to be me. I moved over and lifted up the padlock. It was old but very, very sturdy. "I think I could pick this maybe. . ." I said shakily. "If I had something to pick it with. Do you have anything in your pockets?" I turned to face them all. "A hairpin? Anything like that?" I tried to keep my voice steady, but it was coming out a bit panicky. All three of them shook their heads.

"I have a pencil in my inside jacket pocket," Miss Susan said. "Would that work?"

"No," I shook my head. "Although maybe if we could make it really sharp. . ."

"Oh great," Jenny giggled hysterically, "I was just fancying a bit of light whittling!"

In a flash I remembered that there was something in my own pocket. . . the pencil sharpener that Pym had sent me. I gave a little whoop of excitement and Miss Susan and Jenny looked at me as though I was going mad.

"There's a pencil sharpener in my pocket!" I explained. "Miss Susan, if you come here, can you reach it?" After much twisting and bending ourselves around like elaborate pretzels I was holding the pencil from Miss Susan's pocket and she was holding the sharpener. I've done a lot of strange things in my life, but taking part in a two-person

270

pencil sharpening in a cave filling up with freezing water has to be one of the strangest. Finally, we had exposed a good section of the lead, and the tip was dangerously pointy. The water was up to my waist now, and I was shivering.

"OK," I muttered to myself. "You can do this." There was a good chance I was being a little too optimistic. Picking a lock was delicate work at the best of times, but if I snapped the lead in the pencil we were done for. Gently, I began wiggling the improvised lock pick.

"Hurry up, hurry up!" cried Jack, through chattering teeth. The water was almost up to my chest now, and the weight of the chain meant that we had no chance of swimming.

"Be quiet!" I yelled, tensing as I felt the lead bend a little. There were a few more seconds of fraught silence, and I realized with a horrifying certainty that this plan wasn't going to work.

"I can't do it," I said, tears filling my eyes.

"Yes you can!" Miss Susan's voice was firm. "Poppy Pym, I have seen you do extraordinary things. You can do anything you put your mind to. I know you can do this. I believe in you."

Blinking back the tears that seemed to want to

make an appearance even more now, I took a deep breath and returned to the padlock. The water was so high now that I could no longer see it – I had to rely on my instincts.

"Poppy!" Miss Susan cried as the water reached my neck.

And then, at the last possible moment, I felt the lock spring open in my hands.

CHAPTER THIRTY-FOUR

There was no time to lose! The water was still rising as we wriggled out of the chains. The water was up over my mouth now and with a huge sense of relief I felt the weight of the chain fall from my hands. My wrists were still bound, but I kicked my way to the surface, gasping for air. I saw Miss Susan and Jenny bobbing next to me, but there was no sign of Jack.

"He can't get free of the chain!" Jenny gasped, and she did a neat surface dive, disappearing under the water.

"What should we do?" I turned to Miss Susan, but before we could follow Jenny down under the water, she emerged, dragging Jack Jenkins with her.

"I was a lifeguard for three summers." She grinned at me. I smiled back.

Jack started coughing and spluttering, his face pale.

"We need to get out of the water!" Miss Susan exclaimed. She was right, the cave was filling up so quickly that soon the water would reach the ceiling and there would be no escape.

We all kicked our way through the water as fast as we could, over to the wall at the back of the cave, pulling ourselves on to the top step, and lying, panting on the ground. Our hands were still bound together, but we had to get out of there before the water reached the roof of the cave. Stumbling back into the tunnel we scrambled up the passage as fast as our shaking legs would carry us. The tunnel felt endless, dark and twisting. I bashed into the wall, grazing my elbow, and I felt Miss Susan's hand steadying me. None of us said a word. Finally, after what felt like a lifetime, we reached the wall behind Jenny's bedroom. Pushing at the stones there, the door flew open and the four of us fell into the room beyond.

"Help! Help!" a voice was shouting, and I realized that it was me. There was a thundering sound as footsteps ran up the stairs and down the corridor. The door to the room burst open and standing in front of us was Inspector Hartley.

"What the...?" He gasped at the sight of the four of us, soaking wet, covered in mud and sand and falling through the wall. I had to admit it was probably a bit of a surprise.

"Jenny!" someone screamed, and I realized there were other people in the room, as Agatha and Bernard rushed towards their daughter.

Suddenly there were people everywhere. I wasn't sure exactly what was going on, but someone removed the ropes that were tied around my hands and smothered me in a warm dry blanket. Kip and Ingrid dashed in, pulling me into a big group hug.

"Where have you *been*?!" Kip yelled.

"We were so worried!" Ingrid added more quietly, squeezing me around the shoulders. Tears were spilling down my cheeks now and I felt such a sense of relief at being reunited with my friends. They didn't hate me.

"I'm so sorry! I'm so sorry!" I jabbered as they pulled me into an enormous, warm hug.

The door banged open and Mr Grant strode into the room. He took in the situation at a glance, and

275

then, without a word, he rushed over to Miss Susan and started ... kissing her.

Right on the lips!

For a moment I gawped at them, and caught Kip and Ingrid doing the same, their mouths hanging wide open. Mr Grant was in love with Miss Susan! How had I not spotted that? I wondered. Maybe I wasn't as good a detective as I thought! Mr Grant finally let Miss Susan go, but he wrapped his arm around her shoulder. Her cheeks were very pink, and a big shy smile had crept across her face which she tried to hide with her hand. "Really, Michael," she said in her cool voice but I wasn't fooled; she couldn't hide how pleased she was.

Mrs Crockton arrived then with a tray full of steaming mugs of tea, and I swigged at mine gratefully, warming my hands on the toasty china.

"OK," Inspector Hartley said finally. "I think it's time to fill us in on what's been going on." His grey eyes turned in my direction. "Why do I get the feeling you'll be able to tell us all about it, Miss Pym?"

I tried to look modest, but I couldn't help grinning at this. After all, Inspector Hartley knew that I had solved my fair share of mysteries.

276

"Jack Jenkins kidnapped Jenny," I said and there were shocked gasps from the Booths who were still huddled around a weeping Jenny. Everyone turned to face Jack who was shivering in the corner under a blanket. He looked very green around the edges and he hung his head. "Well, sort of," I added, but catching Jenny's eye I thought maybe that bit of the story could wait until later. "But the real mastermind is Stanley Goodwill. He's obsessed with the castle. He wanted to drive the Booths away so that he would inherit the castle himself. I don't know if he was ever planning to let Jenny go or not, but after me and Miss Susan got involved, too many people knew his secret so he decided to get rid of us." I shuddered here, and Mrs Crockton came and pulled me into a big, safe hug.

"I see. And how, if I might ask," Inspector Hartley continued, "did *you* come to be involved?"

"Oh," I said. "Er, well it's a long story, but we were investigating the mystery of a disappearing smuggler and then I sort of found the room where Miss Susan and Jenny were being kept."

"Disappearing smuggler?" Inspector Hartley raised an eyebrow and made a note in his notebook. "Is this another case I should be involved in?"

"Oh no," I said happily, grinning at Kip and Ingrid who looked back questioningly. "Don't worry, we solved it." I squeezed their hands here. "Plus," I added helpfully, "the smuggler disappeared in 1747, so there's not much you can do about it now."

"Fine," said the inspector mildly, seemingly unsurprised by this. "And now, if you are all feeling a little better, perhaps I could ask – do you know where Stanley Goodwill is now?"

I leapt to my feet. How could I be so stupid?! That cold water must have frozen my brain. In all the relief of escaping a terrible watery death I had allowed the criminal to escape! "He rowed away in a boat!" I said. "He must be on his way back here right now!"

Miss Susan put a hand on my arm. "I think maybe we should *all* go and welcome him ashore..." Our eyes met, and without another word we were both running for the door, down the stairs and heading out of the castle with all the others chasing after us. Down we ran, through the gardens, down the path and through Crumley where the villagers came out to stare at us as if we'd all lost our collective marbles. Rounding the corner of the path I cried, "There he is!"

And there he was. Stanley Goodwill was struggling to pull his boat on to shore. Hearing my cry he turned around, and his eyes widened as he saw the gang of angry people descending on him.

"Noooooo!" he cried, and he began trying to push the boat back out to sea, scrabbling around in the sand.

Miss Susan and I descended.

"Aggggggggh!" I yelled, diving in and catching him around the legs.

"Get off me, you little twerp!" he yelled as he struggled to stay upright, shaking me off and swinging around, ready to aim a hard kick in my direction.

"I rrrreally wouldn't do that!" shouted Miss Susan, and to my astonishment, she punched Stanley Goodwill right in the face, with a very neat right hook. He fell down like a ton of bricks, hitting the water with a mighty splash.

A cheer went up on the shore and Miss Susan stood back, looking a bit surprised at herself. Inspector Hartley waded in behind us, pulling a groggy Stanley out of the water and snapping a pair of handcuffs on him.

Miss Susan turned to face me, and I beamed at her. "That was SO BRILLIANT!" I exclaimed, holding out my hand for a high five.

Shyly, Miss Susan slapped my hand with hers. "Poppy," she said, the breeze whipping her blonde hair around her mud-splattered face, "I think we really need to talk."

CHAPTER THIRTY-FIVE

It was a few hours later before Miss Susan and I got to have our talk. First of all there was the arrest of Stanley Goodwill and the arrival of the local police force. Then me, Miss Susan, Jack and Jenny all had to answer a lot of questions and tell the story of what had happened over and over again. After that I went and had a shower before putting my snuggliest pyjamas on and grabbing an important envelope from the bottom of my rucksack. Then I went inside and knocked on Miss Susan's door.

Miss Susan had changed into her pyjamas as well, and she was combing her damp hair. It was reassuring to see her back to her old, neat self. Even her pyjamas were crisp and white and looked like she had just ironed them. Miss Susan sat on the edge of the bed and patted the duvet next to her. I perched there awkwardly, feeling nervous and tongue-tied.

"Poppy," Miss Susan said, taking a deep breath, "there is something I need to tell you." I sat up straighter and nodded in a way that I hoped was encouraging. Miss Susan fidgeted for a second before getting to her feet. She began pacing in front of me. "What I said to you before..." she said finally, "it was true. I am not your mother."

My heart thudded in my chest. After all we had been through, she still wasn't willing to tell me the truth.

"No, Poppy," Miss Susan said, seeing the hurt in my eyes. "You don't understand. Oh, I've made such a mess of this!" She sat back down on the bed next to me and took my hand. "You see, I'm not your mother ... I'm your aunt."

"What?!" I gasped. Miss Susan nodded. "But ... but ... I know it's you!" I said, "I found your picture!" and I reached into the envelope, pulling out the photograph of Miss Susan holding the baby.

Miss Susan's eyes filled with tears. "Oh, Poppy," she said finally. "You're right, that *is* you in the picture there, but I'm not the one holding you." She pointed to the woman in the picture. "That's my twin sister, Evangeline."

It felt like the room had started spinning. "Evangeline. Evangeline is E!" I muttered. "*That's* my mother?"

"Yes." Miss Susan squeezed my hand.

"And you're ... my aunt?" The word sounded funny. Miss Susan must have thought so as well because she laughed shakily.

"I know," she said, "it's strange for me too."

"But, but, how did this happen?" I asked, my brain trying to catch up with all this new information like a puppy chasing a tennis ball.

Miss Susan squared her shoulders and began to explain. "Evangeline and I," she said, "we didn't always get on terribly well. We might have been twins but we were really very different people. Around the time that you were born we weren't on speaking terms. It's something I bitterly regret." Miss Susan paused here, and rubbed her face. "I didn't know anything about you until after your sixth birthday," she said finally. "I came looking for you, but by then you had a family and a home – a wonderful home, far better than I could give you. I knew it would be selfish to take you away from them so I kept quiet."

I squeezed Miss Susan's hand now, and she squeezed mine back.

"I kept an eye on you," Miss Susan carried on. "I used to come and see the circus perform whenever I could, and I watched you, this amazing, fearless girl. I'd held posts in various schools, and when I started working at Saint Smithen's, I saw an opportunity to help you – and to get to know you a little better. I convinced Miss Baxter to offer you a scholarship to come to the school."

"*You* did that?" I gasped. "Does Miss Baxter know who I am?" I added, letting this sink in.

"No," Miss Susan said. "No one knows. I didn't tell anyone."

"Not even Mr Grant?" I asked, peeking up at her.

Miss Susan's cheeks turned pink again. "Not even Mr Grant," she said.

"I can't believe it!" I exclaimed. "All this time you were my aunt?! I thought you didn't like me!"

Miss Susan grimaced. "Oh, Poppy, I know." She sighed. "I just didn't know how to act. I wasn't sure if I should tell you or not, and I'm not very . . .

good ... at, well, family and *feelings* and things." She shrugged helplessly. "In the end I thought it best to keep my distance. You seemed so happy and I didn't want to mess things up for you."

I sat for a moment, then nodded. "I think I understand," I whispered. Then I remembered something. "Oh, but what about the necklace? Can you tell me more about this?" I asked, reaching into the envelope behind me and pulling out the now familiar piece of jewellery, with its engraved heart-shaped charm and tiny delicate pearls.

Miss Susan really began to cry now, gentle tears running down her cheeks. She reached inside the neck of her pyjama top and pulled out her own identical necklace.

"That's Evangeline's necklace," she whispered. "We had one each. Our father gave them to us when we were about your age. You see the design in the engravings?" Miss Susan pointed to the middle of the heart, and that was when I noticed them – two tiny lowercase Es nestled back-to-back in the middle of the pattern carved there. With shaking hands Miss Susan clasped the necklace around my neck and I felt the cool charm resting against my skin. In all the months I had had the necklace I had never felt comfortable trying it on. Now I realized I might never take it off.

Miss Susan held my hand again, and this time I knew I had to say something, to ask a hard question even though, deep down I already knew the answer.

"Where ... where is she now?" I asked. "Evangeline, I mean, my mother?"

"Oh, Poppy," said Miss Susan tearfully. "I'm so sorry. She died six years ago."

EPILOGUE

"Woah," said Kip.

"Yep." I nodded.

"You thought Miss Susan was your mother... but she's actually your ... aunt?" Ingrid said, dazed.

"Correct," I agreed.

"But your mother is Miss Susan's identical twin?" Kip murmured.

"Right again," I said.

"But she's..." Ingrid trailed off.

"Dead," I said quietly. "That's right."

"Woah," Kip said again.

"I think we'd better stop going in circles," I said, helpfully, settling back into the sofa. The three of us were in the drawing room and I'd spent the last hour filling Kip and Ingrid in on all the gory details I had been holding back for months.

"So *this* is why you've been acting so funny," Ingrid said. "Why didn't you just tell us?"

"I don't know," I said twisting my hands. "I should have told you. It would have been better not to deal with it by myself, I realize that now. But I was just too scared and confused. . ." It was my turn to trail off, but Kip and Ingrid both nodded understandingly.

"And so this is all the stuff your mum left with you?" Kip pointed to the items from the envelope that I had laid out for them to see on the drawing room floor.

"Yes," I said, glancing down at the receipt and the card with the long number on it. The necklace was still around my neck, and I rested my hand against the silver charm.

"So what does it mean?" Kip asked. "'For Emergencies 09325691502763902751'?"

"I don't know," I said, shaking my head. "Miss Susan – Elaine – my aunt . . . didn't know either. I think it must be some kind of code."

"That's SO WEIRD!" Kip exclaimed. "What ARE you going to call Miss Susan now?"

I shrugged. I still wasn't sure what the answer was, and there was definitely a lot more for me and Miss Susan to talk about. Ingrid had picked up the card and was staring at it closely. "What is it, Ing?" I asked.

"Oh, it's nothing..." Ingrid said. "I was just thinking. Could it be a phone number?"

"A phone number?" I said with a frown, a feeling of excitement growing in my tummy. "Isn't it a bit long?"

"Yes, maybe." Ingrid sighed. "I just thought because it says 'for emergencies', you know."

I jumped to my feet. "Well, it's about the only thing I haven't tried. Let's give it a go!" I pointed to the telephone on the table nearby. It took a long time to dial the big string of numbers on the old-fashioned phone, but eventually I had done it. I cradled the receiver to my ear and there was a long silence on the other end of the line. "I don't think anything's happening," I said, disappointed. Just then the phone gave two short sharp rings.

"Sal's Shoe Shop," said a woman who picked up the other end of the phone.

"Oh, yes... Hello," I stuttered. "Um, I wonder if you can help me?"

"Can I please take your order details?" the woman chirped.

I almost dropped the phone. "My – my order details?" I repeated, dazed.

"This is Sal's Shoe Shop," the woman repeated. "Please can I take your order details."

Sal's Shoe Shop. Why did that sound so familiar? And then I remembered: the receipt! "Pass me the receipt!" I hissed, covering the mouthpiece of the phone with my hand. Kip and Ingrid skittered across the floor, in a race to grab it. Kip just about won, and he sprinted back and pressed it into my hand.

"Er, hello," I said into the telephone. "I have a receipt for a pair of pink trainers, size six?"

There was another pause.

"Thank you for your call," said the woman briskly. "Your order has been logged."

And with that the phone went dead.

"What was that all about?" Kip asked.

"I have no idea," I said, "but I think we'd better try and find out."

ACKNOWLEDGEMENTS

The biggest and best thank you as always to my amazing family. Mum and Dad — no one could have more supportive and loving parents. I am so grateful for you and everything you do for us. Also to Harry and Kate with loads of love. Thank you to my EXTRAORDINARY niece and nephew, Imy and Alex, for making being an auntie the greatest job, and to the rest of La Famille Tarte Normande' I raise my (very expensive) glass of Calvados.

A massive thank you to Louise and Gen without whom this book simply could not be. Working with both of you is such a dream and I am so grateful that you share my dedication to good breakfast food and taking the Gilmore Girls way too seriously. To all the utterly brilliant people at Scholastic who somehow manage to turn my scrappy ramblings into the beautiful, sparkling book you hold in your hand — thank you so much. You're the best. Thank you to Liam Drane, designer extraordinaire and Beatrice Bencivenni the amazing illustrator for constantly surprising me with the most beautiful illustrations and for making Poppy's story come to life in a way I couldn't even imagine.

Thanks to a motley crew of PhD survivors who make my life a hundred times more joyful. Mary, Chris, Ben, Nick and Emma – celebratory cheese and tequila soon. And thank you to Paul Grigsby who makes me laugh and always gives me the last chocolate in the box. You're the best thing that ever happened to me.

ABOUT THE AUTHOR

Laura Wood won the inaugural Montegrappa Scholastic Prize for New Children's Writing with her first novel, *Poppy Pym and the Pharaoh's Curse*. Since then, she has been shortlisted for the Sainsbury's Children's Book Award and is currently working on more books in the Poppy Pym series. Laura has recently completed her PhD in English Literature at the University of Warwick. She loves Georgette Heyer novels, Fred Astaire films, travelling to far-flung places, recipe books, cosy woollen jumpers, crisp autumn leaves, new stationery, salted caramel, dogs, and drinking lashings of ginger beer.

Like I said, if you haven't read
my second book you really definitely should.

Look at all of these great reviews!

"FIVE STARS (that shine like Lucas Quest's
beautiful shiny teeth)"
Official pick of the Lucas Quest Fan Club.

"It made me laugh until I threw up."
BoBo the Clown

"This book is even better than the first one"
a character who wasn't in the first book.

(It's spooky and silver and you will totally LOVE it!)

Love, Poppy xx